CONFESSION TO MURDER

First class Scottish crime fiction

ROBERT McNEILL

Published by The Book Folks, London, 2022

Mass market paperback, 2025

ISBN 978-1-80462-318-3

www.thebookfolks.com

Chapter One

They'd been necking for less than a minute when he felt her tongue in his mouth, beneath his – probing, stroking.

Recoiling in disgust, he grasped her throat, placed his thumbs on her larynx, and increased pressure until he closed off her airway.

She gave a strangled cry, and he squeezed harder. Seconds later he heard a faint rattle, and the girl slumped lifeless into the seat beside him.

Making sure the coast was clear, he exited the car and carried her body to the boot. At the city's outskirts he found a narrow track leading off a B road. He stopped after half a mile, dragged her corpse to a grove of trees and covered it with bracken, then retraced his steps and headed back into town.

He'd felt neither guilt nor remorse at the time. But now, more than a week later, he found his actions difficult to come to terms with.

Her French-kissing might have been the catalyst... it was a practice he found abhorrent.

But there'd been something else. Several times in recent months he'd struggled to contain orgasm until after penetration.

And that night it had happened again.

He'd gained an erection, but the moment she took off her knickers, he climaxed in his underpants.

What was the quack term? *Premature ejaculation.* Could this – combined with the unexpected use of her tongue – have pushed him over the edge?

He wasn't sure.

What had surprised him was the *extent* of his anger – and how quickly it had surfaced. Also unsettling had been a feeling of disassociation… almost as if he'd watched someone else do the deed.

He continued walking, one thought uppermost: this detachment, this uncontrolled fury – what were the chances it might re-emerge?

It was a disturbing prospect.

St Bridget's Chapel came into view, and he had a further thought – *should he confide in a priest?*

A lapsed Catholic, he struggled to recall when he'd last been in church. Ten years ago? Twenty? He wracked his brain and it came back to him – his previous confession had taken place when his mother died, a month after his eighteenth birthday.

Nine years earlier.

It had been a relief to unburden his conscience then. He'd agonised over the rift between them; the guilt he had felt when she passed. The confession had removed a weight from his shoulders.

What happened a little over a week ago, however, had been something else.

A priest was able to grant absolution, but for *murder?*

However, there yet might be a saving grace – killing the girl had been totally out of character.

And that prompted the question – had he been a victim of possession? He'd read about satanic spirits that roamed the dark reaches of the night, exerting a malign influence on the susceptible.

Which would explain why he'd felt so detached.

Could a priest really rid such evil? He knew that, acting through God, these men could grant forgiveness – but did they have the power to exorcise demons, too?

He had to pray that they did.

* * *

'Caught up in the roadworks, boss?' DS Bill Fulton was saying. He and his colleagues DS Arlene McCann and DC Mark Hathaway were sitting at their desks in Gayfield Square Police Station and DI Jack Knox had just entered the room.

'Uh-huh,' Knox replied, checking his watch. 'They're resurfacing London Road – how did you know?'

'I drove in that way myself,' Fulton said. 'Caught a report on Radio Forth and diverted via Easter Road and Brunswick Terrace. They're going to be at it all week, apparently.'

Knox shook his head. 'Didn't have the radio on,' he said, nodding to a door at the corner of the room. 'Chief in yet?'

'A couple of minutes ahead of you,' McCann replied, indicating a Styrofoam cup on the desk in front of her. 'Just come from the drinks machine,' she said. 'Brought an extra cup.'

Knox went to his desk, shrugged off his coat and draped it over the back of a chair, and picked up the coffee. 'Cheers, Arlene,' he said. 'You're a lifesaver.' He glanced at Hathaway, who was hunched over a computer. 'Anything cooking, Mark?'

Hathaway looked back at Knox and shook his head. 'Following up inquiries on the missing girl, boss. Uniform spoke to a woman who saw her in a café in Broughton Street on the thirteenth. Nothing since.'

Knox dipped his head in acknowledgement and waved to the DCI's office. 'Did Warburton say anything on his way in?'

Fulton straightened in his chair. 'Only that he wanted a word with me later.'

Knox turned and caught Fulton's look of concern. 'Problem, Bill?'

'Maybe,' Fulton replied. 'A man I arrested at Pik-Pak on Saturday for attempted theft of a mobile phone. Wrestled him to the ground and he broke a rib. His brief's been onto HQ, pleading excessive use of force.'

'Over a broken rib?'

'Wee bit more serious than that. He's in intensive care. It punctured his lung.'

Knox downed the remainder of his coffee and threw the empty cup into a wastebasket. 'Pik-Pak,' he said, 'isn't that the electrical store in Newhaven Road?'

'Yeah,' Fulton confirmed. 'I was there with the wife looking for a new microwave. Old one's on its last legs. We'd narrowed the choice down to two and were debating which one to buy when we heard shouting. I turned and saw the shop security guy arguing with a man in his twenties, name of Gilliland. The guard was asking him to open a holdall. Gilliland told him to F-off.'

'Which is when you stepped in?' Knox asked.

'Aye,' Fulton said. 'Flashed my warrant card and said to do as the guy asked.'

'But Gilliland was having none of it?'

'Exactly,' Fulton replied. 'Dropped the bag, ran for the exit, and I stuck out one of my size tens. He was in the process of getting back onto his elbows when I carried out a half nelson and cuffed him.'

'How'd he break his rib?'

'The way he fell,' Fulton said. 'Caught his left side on the edge of a pallet.'

'The DCI said his brief had contacted Gartcosh?'

'Yep,' Fulton said. 'Told me there was a possibility they might call in Complaints.'

'Wee bit much, don't you think, boss?' McCann said. 'Bill was carrying out a legitimate arrest.'

'Couldn't agree more, Arlene. But if Gilliland's brief's made it official, it'll be taken seriously.'

Fulton gave a rueful nod. 'Especially now the bugger's in ICU.'

'Not to worry, Bill,' McCann said. 'It won't be long before you're in the clear. I'm pretty sure of that.'

McCann had just spoken when the DCI opened the door of his office. Warburton was a tall, distinguished-looking man who carried his height gracefully. He spotted Knox, beckoned, and said, 'Can I have a word, Jack?'

'Sir.' Knox gave Fulton's arm a reassuring tap, then turned and joined his boss.

'Take a pew,' Warburton said as Knox entered. The DCI settled into his own seat, gestured to a telephone on his desk, and added, 'I've just taken a call from head office.'

'Concerning Bill Fulton?'

Warburton stared at Knox for a moment, then gave a look of comprehension. 'Oh, that? They haven't followed up on the Gilliland case yet. Likely they'll be in touch later this morning.' A pause. 'No, this is something else.'

Knox's brow furrowed. 'Sir?'

'A Bishop Edmund O'Malley, Catholic diocese for Edinburgh. Got in touch with head office this morning; it would appear he's a friend of the ACC. O'Malley's call was in connection with one of his priests – Father Ryan Murphy at St Bridget's in Bonnington Road. Murphy took a confession yesterday from a man who confessed to killing a girl. Some outlandish tale about his being possessed; wanted the priest to exorcise his demons.'

'This girl,' Knox said. 'Did the man tell Murphy who it was?'

'Apparently not. Slipped out of the confessional soon after Murphy told him he was unable to perform an exorcism. Advised the man to turn himself in.'

'Did Murphy or anyone else get a look at him?'

'Only the church deacon. Described him as dark-haired, medium height, late twenties or early thirties.'

'This happened yesterday,' Knox said. 'Why didn't the bishop contact us sooner?'

'Father Murphy,' Warburton replied. 'He was worried about breaking the confessional seal. Wrestled with his conscience overnight; phoned O'Malley this morning.'

'Did Murphy say how the woman was murdered?'

'The ACC asked, but it appears not. The man was in the confessional for only a few minutes. When Murphy mentioned police, he made himself scarce.'

'So, a killer's confession is all we have. No indication of who the victim was or where she was murdered?'

Warburton shook his head. 'No, that's it,' he said. 'Always possible the man is a fantasist; that there was no murder.'

'Mm-hmm,' Knox said. 'I'm not so sure. We've had a missing girl on our books since a week past Friday.'

'Laura Winter, the Canadian?' Warburton picked up a folder and opened it. 'Says here that Inspector Guthrie from our Queen Charlotte Street office checked it out.' He tapped the page. 'Guthrie's of the opinion she might have left Edinburgh. She'd paid the B&B in advance.'

'I know, sir,' Knox said. 'But it's strange that she laid out for five days, yet only stayed three.'

Warburton shrugged. 'Well, the ACC has asked us to speak to Murphy ASAP – you'll see him?'

Knox rose and turned towards the door. 'Of course,' he said.

'And Jack?'

'Sir?'

'Have DS McCann accompany you. I'd like DS Fulton to stay in the office, in case Complaints decide to interview him today.'

Chapter Two

'This girl, Laura Winter,' McCann was saying. 'She was staying in Leith?'

Knox had turned into Pilrig Street from Leith Walk and slowed for a taxi ahead, which braked suddenly and double-parked outside a hotel, its hazard lights flashing.

'Oh, I forgot, Arlene, you were on leave last week,' he replied. 'Yes, she's from Ontario, aged twenty-one. Booked into the Sea View Guest House in Links Place on Wednesday, 11 March and paid five days in advance. Departed after breakfast three days later and didn't return.'

'Inspector Guthrie thinks she left the city?'

Knox waited for an approaching lorry, and overtook the cab. 'Uh-huh,' he replied. 'Mrs Carter, the guest house owner, said the girl told her she intended sightseeing in the Western Isles. He's guessing she moved on, forgot to mention it to the proprietress.'

'Strange,' McCann said. 'Laura was on her own?'

'Aye. Told Mrs Carter she was a secretary in the Canadian civil service, visiting Scotland for two weeks. She arrived at Edinburgh Airport the same day she booked into the Sea View.'

'The B&B woman alerted us when she didn't come back?'

Knox shook his head. 'No, she did nothing. It was the Ontario police who got in touch the following Monday. Laura's mother contacted them when her daughter didn't e-mail her on the Saturday, as she expected. The girl wasn't answering her mobile, either.' Knox paused, and added, 'Guthrie thinks that's because of her destination – apparently there's a poor internet and mobile connection on some of the islands.'

'But you think there's more to it?'

'I do. You heard Mark say this morning that she was seen by a woman at a café in Broughton Street. That was at 4.30pm. If she'd been heading to the Highlands, she'd have left the city by then.'

Knox indicated right at the next set of traffic lights, turned into Bonnington Road, and drove a short distance and parked.

St Bridget's Roman Catholic Church was a modern building situated at the rear of a wide lawn. Knox and McCann exited the car, and were walking along a pathway leading to the church when they heard a voice behind them.

'Inspector Knox?'

The detectives turned and saw a man in his late forties. His hair was styled in a crew-cut and he was wearing a dog collar.

'Yes,' Knox said. 'You're Father Murphy?'

'Yeah,' the man replied, thumbing over his shoulder. 'I'm staying in a rented apartment in the next block. Saw your car pull up.'

Knox nodded and gestured towards his colleague. 'This is Detective Sergeant McCann.'

They shook hands and McCann said, 'You're American?'

Murphy smiled. 'That obvious, huh? Yeah, I'm from Boston. On a six-month exchange visit from St Benedict's in my home city.' He nodded to the entrance. 'Please, come inside. My office is to the right of the vestibule.'

The detectives followed him along a short hallway. Murphy stopped at the entrance to his office and waved them inside, indicating two chairs arranged near a plain wooden desk.

'Please,' he said, 'take a seat.'

Knox and McCann did so, and Murphy walked to the other side of the desk and sat facing them. 'When you phoned you told me Bishop O'Malley had spoken to one of Police Scotland's senior officers,' he said. 'Did he explain what had happened?'

'At the confession, you mean?' Knox asked.

'Yeah.'

'Yes, we were told he had admitted to murdering a young woman; claimed he'd been possessed.'

Murphy nodded. 'I see. Okay, well maybe it would be better if I started at the beginning.'

Knox inclined his head in agreement. 'I think so, Father.'

Murphy gestured towards the door. 'Peter Irving, the deacon, saw the man enter shortly after two yesterday afternoon. The morning service had been held and the church was empty, except for Peter himself and Mrs Docherty, a lady who arranges flowers for evening service. Oh, and two parishioners waiting to take confession.'

'You saw them first?' Knox asked.

'Yes,' Murphy said. 'But it only took five minutes to do both. When the second confessor left, Peter escorted the man to the confessional box.'

'By the way,' Knox said, 'may we speak to Mr Irving before we leave?'

'I anticipated that you'd want to,' Murphy said. 'He's in the sacristy at the moment. I told him I'd call him into the office after we've spoken.'

'Thank you,' Knox said, adding, 'sorry, you were about to tell us what happened when the man entered the confessional?'

'Yes,' Murphy said. 'After he'd taken a seat, he told me it had been nine years since his last confession, and I asked him to go ahead. He said, "I've taken the life of a young woman, Father."

'He said it in such a quiet tone of voice that I wasn't sure I'd heard correctly. I asked him to repeat and he told me, "It happened in the early hours of Saturday. I was with a young woman. We were sitting in the back seat of my car, necking..." He fell silent for a moment or two, and continued, "If she hadn't..."

'"Hadn't what?" I asked.

'"Cataglottis," he said. "If she hadn't initiated the act, I don't think it would have happened."'

Murphy saw the blank look on Knox and McCann's faces, and said, 'I know: it's a ten-dollar word I hadn't heard before either. I had to check the dictionary. It means French kissing.'

'Ah,' Knox said. 'What happened then?'

'Just to make sure I hadn't misheard, I asked, "Did you just say you'd taken someone's life?"

'"My hands carried out the deed, Father," he said. "But it wasn't me. It's not in my character. I've been the victim of satanic possession, which is why I've come to plead with you. Please exorcise this evil from my soul."'

'How did you respond?' Knox asked.

'I told him I was sorry. Exorcism wasn't something I was qualified to do. I paused a moment to let that sink in, and added, "I think it's possible you're ill, my son, and I suggest you go to the police and confess."

'"You won't even grant absolution?" he said.

'"Not for murder, I'm afraid, no," I replied.

'He was quiet for a moment or two, then his voice rose. "You think I'm some kind of nut-job, don't you? What

I've told you is a cock and bull story to help salve my conscience?"

"'I'm not here to judge," I replied. "I only suggest you go to the police because it's the right thing do. If you're in need of professional help, they'll make sure you get it." I heard nothing and waited a moment or two, then added, "You do understand, don't you?"'

'When he didn't reply, I glanced at the grill separating us and saw light coming in from the door on his side. It took a few seconds for me to gather some items from my lap, and when I exited the confessional, he had gone.'

'He'd left the church completely?' Knox asked.

'Yes.'

'I see,' Knox said, then paused for a moment, and added, 'How long have you been in Edinburgh, Father?'

'Four months. Why?'

'The reason I'm asking is because of my next question.'

'Go ahead.'

'Are you able to tell if he had a local accent?'

Murphy smiled. 'Oh, that. Yeah, it was a bit of a challenge at first for me to understand the local dialect – particularly that of ordinary folks. I'd have to ask people to speak slowly in order to understand them. Didn't take long to pick it up, though. You were wondering if he came from the city?'

'Yes.'

'I'd say so, yeah.'

'Middle-class?'

'Uh-huh, quite well spoken. Pretty well educated, too, I think.'

McCann nodded. 'Yes,' she said. 'Given the word he used to describe French kissing.'

Murphy grinned. 'Quite.'

'One more thing,' Knox said. 'You didn't see him at any point during the confession?'

'No, sorry. As I've told you, I was already seated in the confessional box when Peter brought him to me. The grill in the partition is made of very fine mesh. If you look hard you can see an outline of the person on the other side, but I don't think most priests, myself included, ever bother.'

Knox scribbled a few lines into his notebook and nodded, 'Thank you, Father, that's been very helpful.' He pointed to the office entrance. 'Would you be so kind as to ask Mr Irving to come in?'

Murphy rose and went to the door. 'Of course,' he said. 'I'll go and get him.'

As the priest left the room McCann motioned towards the window. 'I had a wee look as we approached the church,' she said. 'Didn't see any CCTV.'

Knox nodded. 'I'd say the chances are slim. Mostly residential flats this end of Bonnington Road.'

'I don't suppose the church has one, either?'

'Unlikely.'

The door opened at that moment and Father Murphy reappeared together with a portly man in his sixties. 'This is Peter Irving,' he said. 'Our deacon. Peter, these are the detectives – DI Knox and DS McCann.'

Irving made a slight bow and said, 'Pleased to meet you.'

'Right,' Murphy said. 'Take my chair, Peter, and I'll leave you to it.' Then, to the detectives, he added, 'If you need to see me again before you go, officers, I'll be at the ambry; other side of the altar.'

Knox dipped his head in response and said, 'Thank you, Father.'

As Murphy left, Irving sat hesitantly, glanced nervously at the detectives and adjusted a pair of wire-framed spectacles on the bridge of his nose. 'Not sure how much help I can be,' he said. 'I'm not awfully good at faces.'

'It's okay,' Knox said reassuringly. 'Just tell us what you remember.' A pause. 'Father Murphy told us the man entered the church a little after two?'

'Yes,' Irving replied. 'I can be sure of that because it was soon after Mrs Docherty arrived to do the floral arrangements. She's always prompt.'

'I see,' Knox said. 'And where were you when the man entered the church?'

'In the nave. Sorting bibles for evening service.'

'And the others waiting to take confession,' McCann said. 'Where were they seated?'

'In the rear pews, opposite the confessional.'

'You hadn't seen him before?' Knox asked.

'No,' Irving replied. 'And I can say that with certainty.' Irving smiled. 'I appear to be contradicting myself, don't I? Telling you I'm not good with faces? I recognise most of our regular parishioners, of course.'

'How old would you say he was?' Knox said.

'Young. Late twenties or early thirties. Average build, dark-haired. A head or so taller than myself – I'm five foot seven.'

'More than six feet?'

'I think so, yes.'

'How was he dressed?'

Irving's brow wrinkled. 'Let me see… dark suit. Navy or dark charcoal. I think he might have been wearing a tie, but I'm not sure.'

'His face,' Knox said. 'Any distinguishing features?'

'Nothing that stood out.'

'Clean shaven?'

'Yes.'

'The nave,' McCann said. 'That's the main body of the church?'

'Yes.'

'And you didn't go to him – he approached you?'

'Yes. He walked straight up to me and said, "I'd like to take confession." I asked him to take a seat near the two women who were waiting. Told him I'd escort him to the confessional box when it became his turn.'

'After he took his seat, you returned to the nave?' Knox asked.

'I did, yes. But kept a clear line of sight between me and the confessional box. So that when someone exited, I was able to take the next confessor over.'

'And when his turn came, he was the only one waiting?'

'Yes.'

'Did he speak again when you took him to Father Murphy?'

'No, he followed me in silence.'

'And after he entered the box, you returned to the nave?'

'Yes.'

'Father Murphy told us the man was with him for only a couple of minutes, then left abruptly. Did you see him leave?'

'I did, yes. Though by that time Mrs Docherty had asked me for a watering can and I'd gone to a cupboard near the apse to fetch it. On my return I saw him exit the confessional and walk quickly back to the entrance.'

'Father Murphy told us the man spoke with a local accent, which he thought was middle class,' McCann said. 'Would you agree?'

'He sounded like he came from a better-off background, yes.'

'Did Mrs Docherty see the man?' Knox asked.

'I asked her, but she said no. She told me she'd paid no attention to the folk waiting to take confession. Her focus had been on the flowers.'

'What happened after the man left?'

'Father Murphy beckoned me over and asked if I'd seen him leave, which I confirmed. He told me he'd left the confessional unexpectedly. Both of us went outside to check.'

'You didn't see him?'

'No,' Irving replied. 'He'd disappeared.'

Chapter Three

Fulton had finished drying his hands on the hot-air machine and was leaving the toilet when he was intercepted by Hathaway, who nodded towards Warburton's office. 'Two guys came in while you were in the bog,' he said. 'Asked for the DCI – they've not long gone in.'

'Complaints?' Fulton asked.

'I think so.'

'They say who they were?'

'A DCI Collins and a DI who introduced himself as Simms… or it might've been Simmonds. He was soft-spoken – not sure I heard him right.'

'What'd they look like?'

'Collins carrying a bit of weight, around fifty; seemed amiable enough. The DI more poker-faced. Thirtyish, sports a thin moustache.'

'Collins asked for Warburton by name?'

'Yeah.'

Fulton glanced at his watch. 'Hmm,' he said. 'Half past twelve. I was hoping they'd wait until after lunch.'

As Fulton spoke, the door to Warburton's office opened and his boss exited together with two men.

Warburton motioned towards Fulton and indicated the man at his side. 'DS Fulton,' he said. 'This is Detective Chief Inspector Reginald Collins, Professional Standards Department. His colleague is Detective Inspector Dave Simmonds. Both officers will be interviewing you regarding Mr Gilliland.'

Collins extended his hand. 'Pleased to meet you, DS Fulton,' he said pleasantly. 'DCI Warburton advised that you're entitled to have a Federation rep sit in on the interview?'

Fulton shook his hand and said, 'Yes, sir, he did, but I don't think there'll be any need.'

Collins nodded. 'I see, Sergeant. Your prerogative, of course.' He turned to Warburton. 'Interview room 2 you said, Ronald?'

The DCI dipped his head and gestured towards the entrance. 'Yes. Left along the corridor outside. Second on the right.'

A few moments later Fulton and the Professional Standards detectives were seated in the interview room, Collins and Simmonds on one side of the desk, Fulton on the other.

Collins checked his watch, then glanced at Fulton and said, 'I know it's almost lunch time, Sergeant, so we'll endeavour to keep this as short as possible.'

He nodded to Simmonds, who opened the briefcase he was carrying and handed over a folder, which Collins took and lay flat on the table. He extracted a pair of spectacles from his jacket pocket, and put them on. He read through the document in silence for a few seconds and nodded to Simmonds again, who switched on a NEAL recording machine.

'You know why we're here, Sergeant Fulton,' Collins said, 'but for the benefit of the tape I have to read you a complaint filed by Miles Read, a solicitor acting on behalf of Edward Gilliland, who sustained serious injury while you carried out his arrest on Saturday, 21 March at the Pik-

Pak store on Newhaven Road. Mr Read claims you used excessive force in the execution of his client's arrest. You're aware of the nature of the allegation?'

Fulton shifted uncomfortably in his chair. 'I am, sir, yes,' he said.

Collins dipped his head in acknowledgement. 'Very well then, we'll proceed.' Collins lay his hands flat on the folder and added, 'We'll start from the beginning. You say in your statement you were in the Pik-Pak store when your attention was drawn to an altercation between Mr Gilliland and Bernard Wilkie, a member of the security staff – would you care to take it from there?'

'Yes, sir,' Fulton replied. He nodded towards the folder. 'As mentioned in my statement, my wife and I were there looking to buy a new microwave – our old one's knackered, you see.'

Collins gave an indulgent smile. 'Uh-huh, carry on.'

'All of a sudden I heard raised voices,' Fulton continued. 'I looked down the aisle and saw a rammy had broken out between the security lad and Gilliland.'

Simmonds looked directly at Fulton and spoke for the first time. 'You mean Mr Wilkie?'

'Yes.'

'Go on.'

'Well the security lad – Mr Wilkie – insisted Gilliland open a holdall he was carrying. Gilliland became aggressive, told Wilkie to F-off.'

'What happened then?' Collins asked.

'I heard Wilkie say something to the effect that he suspected Gilliland had yanked a mobile phone from the unit where it was displayed, breaking the cord securing it.'

'"Something to the effect",' Simmonds said, a hint of sarcasm in his voice.

Fulton gave the DI a piercing stare. 'Aye,' he said. 'I wasn't close enough to hear it word-for-word.'

'Which was when you intervened?' Collins asked.

'Yes, I went to where they were standing, took out my warrant card, and showed it to Gilliland. Told him to open the holdall.'

'And did he?' Simmonds said.

'Well, he gave me a blank look, bent down, and I thought he was going to comply. But suddenly he grabbed the bag and made a breenge for the door.'

'How near were you at this point?' Collins asked.

'Maybe three or four feet.'

'I see. Carry on.'

'It was just a reflex,' Fulton said. 'I stuck out my foot and he tripped over it.'

'Where did he fall?' Simmonds asked.

Fulton gave the DI a blank look. 'I'm not sure what you mean.'

'Mr Gilliland's injury was caused by him coming in contact with a pallet at the edge of the aisle,' Simmonds said. 'Is that where he fell?'

'Must've done,' Fulton replied.

'He attempted to get up?' Collins asked.

'Jumped to his feet almost right away,' Fulton replied. I wrestled him to the ground and put the cuffs on him.'

'You wrestled him to the ground,' Simmonds said. 'How exactly?'

'Put him in a half nelson,' Fulton replied. 'Then subdued him and placed him under arrest.'

'Isn't it possible, Sergeant Fulton,' Simmonds said, 'that Gilliland actually fell into the centre of the aisle, and that he came into contact with the pallet after you tackled him?'

'No, it isn't,' Fulton said. 'He was nowhere near the pallets then.'

'My point is,' Simmonds retorted, 'would he have been so quick to rise if he'd already sustained a life-threatening injury?'

Fulton shot the DI an angry look, but said nothing.

Collins addressed Fulton in a conciliatory tone of voice. 'You're aware that we're trying to establish if *unnecessary* force was used in Gilliland's apprehension,' he said. 'You don't think his rib was broken as a consequence of your actions?'

'No,' Fulton said emphatically. 'Why not ask Wilkie? He was there.'

Simmons gave a thin smile. 'We did,' he said. 'He says he isn't sure if Gilliland came into contact with the pallets as a result of the fall, or due to the manner of his arrest.'

Fulton shook his head. 'Gilliland was nowhere near the pallets when I nabbed him.'

Collins dipped his head in acknowledgement. 'As DI Simmonds says, we spoke to Wilkie, but there are two other members of staff who witnessed the incident we've yet to interview. A shelf-stacker and a salesman who were off duty this morning. We'll speak to them later today.' He tapped the folder and flashed Fulton a brief but encouraging smile. 'So our inquiries aren't concluded. They might be able to offer corroboration that puts you in the clear.'

Fulton gave a nod of acceptance and said, 'How is Gilliland, sir?'

Collins returned the folder to Simmonds, who replaced it in his briefcase. 'Still serious when I checked this morning, but holding up,' he replied. 'His doctors say if he makes it through the next couple of days there's a chance he'll recover.

'However, you understand, Sergeant Fulton, that excessive use of force is something the Chief Constable takes a dim view of. Places all of us in a bad light, particularly if it gets into the media, which it is wont to do.'

'Yes, sir,' Fulton said. 'But I can only repeat, no undue force was used in Gilliland's arrest.'

The pair got to their feet. 'Okay, that'll do for now,' Collins said. 'I'll ask DCI Warburton to keep you on administrative duties until the outcome of our findings. Later this week, most likely.'

* * *

McCann nodded to their surroundings when they got back in the car. 'You were right, boss,' she said. 'No sign of CCTV anywhere.'

Knox placed his iPhone on the dash mount and scrolled through its address book. 'There's a business estate at the bottom end that might have a few cameras. No guarantee he went that way, of course.'

'You think he's local?'

'Possible. Or knows the area, at least. Why he picked St Bridget's.'

McCann clicked her belt into the anchor point. 'Links Place, that's near here, isn't it?'

'Five-minute drive,' Knox replied. He shot McCann a sidelong glance and smiled. 'You're reading my thoughts?'

'Laura Winter. You think she's fallen victim to our penitent?'

Knox found the number he was looking for and pressed *call*. 'Uh-huh,' he replied. 'I'm giving Guthrie a ring, see if he has anything new to tell us.'

The detectives heard the dial tone reverberate through the speakers, then a man's voice answered, 'Leith Police Station, Sergeant Adams speaking, how can I help you?'

'DI Knox, Gayfield Square,' Knox replied. 'Is DI Guthrie in his office?'

'I think so, sir,' Adams replied. 'You want to speak to him?'

'Please.'

'Wait a sec – I'll buzz you through.' There was a momentary hum of static, then Guthrie came on the line. 'Morning, Jack,' he said. 'What can I do for you?'

'Morning, Tam. I'm calling about Laura Winter, the missing Canadian girl. I was wondering if you'd heard anything?'

'No, I haven't,' Guthrie said. 'We appear to have hit a bit of a dead end. The Highland boys checked hotels and B&Bs in the Western Isles and asked operators if anyone matching her description had been seen on the ferries. Came up empty.'

'You know she was spotted at the Toddle Inn café in Broughton Street at 4.30pm a week past Friday?' Knox said.

'Oh, that,' Guthrie replied. 'False trail, I'm afraid. One of my DSs, Joe Buckley, ran it down. Turns out the woman – who admittedly looks like the Winter girl – was a lassie who works at a hairdressers in Rodney Street. Buckley simply forgot to update the computer.'

'So you're winding it up?'

'There's nothing much else I can do at the moment. Highland Constabulary have passed her details to plods in the outer isles and further north; see what develops. Till then, we'll pretty much have to sit on it. I'm curious, though – why are you asking?'

'I'm in the process of investigating a man who confessed to a priest that he strangled a girl,' Knox said. 'I think there might be a connection.'

'Did the priest say where this happened?'

'That's just it. The man didn't tell him.'

Guthrie snorted in derision. 'Christ, Jack. One of the hallmarks of an attention-seeking nutter. You and I have come across plenty in our time.'

'Normally I'd agree, Tam,' Knox said, 'but I'm not so sure here. I'd like to dig a bit deeper. You mind if I speak to Mrs Carter at the Sea View B&B – check it out?'

'Not at all, Jack,' Guthrie said. 'Be my guest.'

Chapter Four

The Sea View Guest House was situated two-thirds of the way along a row of villas facing a wide stretch of parkland known as Leith Links. Knox and McCann walked up a short pathway, where Knox's ringing of the doorbell was answered by a woman in her late fifties.

'Mr and Mrs Walker?' she said, looking surprised. 'I really must apologise – your room's not ready yet.'

'You're Mrs Carter?' Knox asked.

'Yes.'

'I think you're confusing us with someone else,' Knox said. He took out his warrant card and showed it to her. 'DI Knox and DS McCann. We're here in connection with Laura Winter, the young woman who stayed with you the week before last.'

'Oh, I'm sorry,' she said. 'A couple phoned late last night and made a reservation. I told them to wait until after one. I thought that's who you were.' She paused for a moment and her brow furrowed. 'The Canadian girl's still missing? I was led to believe she'd gone to the Hebrides.'

'I'm afraid she hasn't,' Knox said, and indicated the hallway behind her. 'May we come in and ask a couple of questions? We won't keep you long.'

The woman opened the door and waved them inside. 'Of course,' she said. 'The lounge is on the right.'

The detectives entered the room, followed by Mrs Carter, who gestured to a settee opposite the fireplace. 'Please,' she said. 'Take a seat.'

Knox and McCann did so and the proprietress took an armchair opposite. 'I don't know if I can add anything to what I told Detective Inspector Guthrie last week,' she said. 'He spoke to me at length. Willie, too.'

'Willie?' McCann said.

'My son, he runs the guest house with me – he booked Ms Winter in.'

'Your son,' Knox said. 'He's here?'

Mrs Carter nodded. 'In the kitchen. You want me to get him?'

'If you don't mind,' Knox replied.

Mrs Carter rose and left the room, and moments later Knox and McCann heard the murmur of voices at the rear of the guest house, including that of a male who sounded annoyed.

Soon afterwards Mrs Carter reappeared with a muscular-looking man in his mid-thirties. He glanced briefly at the detectives and said, 'I really don't see why you'd want to go over all this again. We told the Leith police officers all we know.'

'I understand,' Knox said. 'But we're in the process of following another lead and want to make sure nothing's been missed. As I said to Mrs Carter, we'll only take a few minutes of your time.'

The man looked at his mother, then back at Knox. 'Okay,' he said resignedly. 'If you think it'll help.'

'Thank you,' Knox said. A pause, then, 'Your mother told us it was you who saw Ms Winter when she arrived?'

'Yes,' Carter said, 'I answered the doorbell. Mum was upstairs, hoovering one of the bedrooms.'

'This was on Wednesday, 11 March?'

'Yes.'

'What time of day?' McCann asked.

'A little after 5pm.'

'Ms Winter,' Knox said. 'She'd already booked?'

'No, I think the tourist board at Waverley sent her; they'd phoned an hour earlier to ask if we'd any vacancies.' He turned to his mother, who was in the process of settling back into her armchair. 'Mum?'

She dipped her head in agreement. 'Yes, they rang a wee while before. Didn't confirm, though, so she really wasn't expected.'

'Inspector Guthrie told us she paid for five days?' Knox asked.

'Yes,' Mrs Carter said. 'In advance. Wednesday evening until the following Monday morning.'

'But only stayed until Friday?' McCann asked.

'Yes.'

'She told you she was going?'

Mrs Carter shook her head. 'No, not a word.'

'What about her luggage?' Knox asked.

'She was travelling light,' her son said. 'The only thing she had with her was a backpack.'

'You saw her leave?' Knox asked.

'No,' Carter said. 'I'd left for the cash and carry just after eight. Didn't get back till after ten.' He glanced at his mother. 'You didn't either, did you, Mum?'

'No,' Mrs Carter said. 'I was tidying one of the rooms.'

'Did you do her room afterwards?' McCann asked.

Mrs Carter nodded. 'Yes, changed the sheets and gave it a general clean.'

'You didn't notice if her backpack had gone?'

'Can't say I did. In fact, nothing looked out of place. There was a box of tissues on the dresser, with some toiletries and cosmetics.'

'When did you realise she was gone?' Knox asked.

'Only when she didn't come down for breakfast on Saturday. I checked her room and saw her bed hadn't been slept in.'

'And even then we weren't sure,' her son said. 'Occasionally we get folk who stay out overnight. It wasn't until Sunday we realised she'd left.'

'You noticed then that her backpack had gone?'

Carter dipped his head in confirmation. 'Yes.'

'But the toiletries and cosmetics were still there?'

'Yes,' Mrs Carter replied.

'You don't think it odd that she left without them?'

She shook her head. 'Not really,' she said. 'You'd be surprised at the things people leave behind.'

'Inspector Guthrie said you thought she was headed for the Western Isles,' Knox said. 'She mentioned this to you?'

'At breakfast the day after she arrived,' Mrs Carter said. 'I chatted to her for a while. She told me she was in Scotland for two weeks. After the weekend she intended travelling to Ardrossan, where she'd get a ferry for Arran. She'd stay there a night or two and head to the Western Isles via Kintyre.'

'She went out afterwards?'

'After breakfast on Thursday?' Mrs Collins said. 'Yes.'

'What was she wearing?' McCann asked.

'She had on a navy jumper when she came down to breakfast; cable knit. Oh, and a thick yellow parka when she went out.' Mrs Carter gave an involuntary shiver. 'You know how cold it's been lately.'

'Did you notice anything else?'

'Uh-huh. Dark-blue jeans – and brown ankle boots, suede.'

'She was out all day?' McCann said.

'Yes,' her son said. 'Got back around seven. I spoke with her here in the lounge when she came down from her room. She told me she'd been doing the usual things; visiting the castle, Royal Mile and Holyrood Palace; Princes Street.'

'Did she talk about meeting anyone else; friends, relatives or the like?' Knox asked.

'No. I got the impression she was on her own.'

'Were other guests present when you spoke to her?'

'Yes,' Carter said. 'One of our regulars, a travelling rep for a carpet company in Leeds.'

'Ms Winter was in conversation with him?'

'Yes, they appeared to be getting along fine.'

'This traveller,' McCann said. 'How old is he?'

'Mr Peabody?' Carter replied. 'Late forties, I think.'

'Did either of you speak to Ms Winter on the day she left?'

'Only a few words at breakfast,' Mrs Carter replied. 'The weather, that sort of thing.'

'This Mr Peabody,' Knox said. 'It's possible Ms Winter said something to him that might be of interest. You don't happen to have his contact details?'

'I do, as it happens,' Carter said. 'He left a couple of his business cards.' He went to a writing desk near the window, opened a drawer, and retrieved a card, which he gave to Knox.

'Much obliged,' Knox said. He and McCann rose then and he added, 'And we're grateful to you both for your cooperation.'

The pair escorted the detectives to the entrance, where Mrs Carter shook her head. 'Well, I can only hope we've been of some help,' she said. 'And that you discover Ms Winter's whereabouts before long.'

Chapter Five

'Fits the description all right,' DI Ed Murray was saying. 'Female; late teens, early twenties.' A few minutes had passed since the detectives left the Sea View, and Knox answered his mobile and heard the forensics officer's voice.

Murray explained that he and his partner, DS Liz Beattie, had been called to a wood ten miles south of Edinburgh, where a young woman's body had been found.

Knox placed his phone on the dash mount and switched to the speakers. 'What was she wearing, Ed?' he said.

'A jumper, navy blue,' Murray said. 'But she was naked from the waist down. Liz and officers from the Dalkeith Police Station undertook a preliminary search of the surrounding area. Found several items of clothing in bushes nearby – they appear to have been put there by her or whoever killed her: dark blue jeans, a yellow parka and ankle-length brown boots.'

'Tallies with what we were told,' Knox said.

'She's been missing since the thirteenth?' Murray asked.

'Yes,' Knox replied. 'Friday morning.'

'Well, the condition of the body bears that out,' Murray said. 'Looks to have been here around ten days: bloating of the abdomen, greenish-black tinge to the skin. Typical of molecular decomposition.'

'The pathologist's there with you?'

'Mr Turley? Not yet. Should be along shortly, though. I phoned his office as soon as we were notified. They rang back fifteen minutes ago, told me he was on his way.'

'Where are you exactly?' Knox asked.

'Cranston Woods. Three miles south of Pathhead on the A68. I'll ping you the coordinates.'

'Fine, Ed,' Knox said, and glanced at his watch. 'It's just gone twelve. DS McCann and I are at Links Place. Just interviewed the Carters, owners of the guest house where Ms Winter was staying. Reckon we'll be with you in half an hour.'

Knox ended the call, tapped the screen of his iPhone and scrolled through some pages, and turned to McCann. 'Just as well you asked what she was wearing, Arlene,' he said. 'Guthrie's notes mention a fleece jacket, but omit its colour, or the fact she was wearing jeans and suede boots.'

McCann nodded. 'What are your thoughts on the backpack?' she asked. 'Curious neither Mrs Carter nor her son saw it had gone.'

'On Friday morning?' Knox said.

'Yeah.'

Knox turned the key in the ignition and the Passat's engine fired. 'Uh-huh,' he said. 'I thought that strange, too.'

* * *

Knox checked the sat nav, indicated left, and drove down a rough track until he came upon a taped-off section manned by a young policeman. He stopped and exited the car, and the officer indicated a stand of pines a hundred yards farther on.

'DI Murray and the others are waiting at the other side of those trees, sir,' he said, addressing Knox. 'He told me to expect you.'

'Do you know if the pathologist's arrived?' Knox said.

'Yes, sir. Fifteen minutes ago.'

Knox acknowledged this with a nod, and he and McCann donned protective coveralls and went to the scene. A tent had been erected and Murray and Beattie were examining some bushes nearby.

Murray looked up as Knox approached and looked at his watch. 'Made nice time, Jack,' he said.

'The roads were quiet,' Knox replied. He gestured towards the tent and added, 'Mr Turley's with the body?'

'Yes,' Murray replied. 'His initial examination agrees with ours: the deceased's been in situ for ten or eleven days.'

'These bushes,' Knox said, 'that's where her clothing was found?'

'Aye,' Murray replied. 'Liz and I were giving them another check.'

At that moment his red-haired companion emerged from behind the thicket. She saw Knox and McCann and said, 'Afternoon, boss. Arlene.'

The detectives returned her greeting, then McCann nodded to an item Beattie was holding. 'Is that what I think it is?' she said.

Beattie placed the specimen in an evidence bag and inclined her head in acknowledgment. 'Ladies' briefs, yes,' she said. 'We missed them earlier.'

'Dumped like the rest of her gear, most likely,' Murray said. 'Don't think her killer deliberately attempted to hide anything.'

Knox thumbed towards the tent. 'She was found in the open?'

'Some loose bits of bracken covered the body,' Murray said. 'Half-hearted attempt at concealment. It seems the killer was in a hurry.'

'Tyre tracks?' Knox asked.

'Why I asked uniform to stop you further down,' Murray said. 'We've a reasonably fresh set of impressions a few yards from here.'

Knox nodded. 'Who discovered her?'

'Farm worker called McGivney,' Murray said. 'Or rather his dog did. Just after ten this morning.' Murray pointed to a stretch of ground at the other side of the tent. 'He was on a path near his cottage at the far end of that field. The dog rooted about, began barking, and McGivney came over and found her.'

Knox's attention was suddenly diverted to the tent, whose flysheet was pulled to one side and a stocky man in his late fifties emerged.

'Afternoon, Alex,' Knox said.

'Afternoon, Jack,' Turley replied. The pathologist gave a mournful look, glanced back, and added, 'This job definitely doesn't get easier.' He shook his head. 'Just a slip of a lass.'

Knox motioned towards the tent. 'Ed told me you confirmed she'd been here more than a week?'

'Aye,' Turley said. 'Ten days or so. I'll be able to say for sure once I perform the PM.'

'Cause of death?' Knox asked.

'Strangulation,' Turley replied. 'No question. Whoever did it squeezed the life out of her.'

'The confessor,' McCann said.

Seeing Turley's baffled expression, Knox explained about the interview with Father Murphy, and the man who'd confessed at St Bridget's.

'Well, he didn't kill her here, I can tell you that,' Turley said. 'Just a guess until I conduct a more in-depth examination, but lividity suggests she died at least an hour earlier.'

'Sexual assault?' Knox asked.

The pathologist shook his head. 'Vaginal swab came up negative, and there's no sign of her disrobing unwillingly.

Can't say for sure until I get her back to the Cowgate, of course, but forcible removal of tights and underwear quite often leave scratch marks. No indication of that here.' Turley pursed his lips. 'No, I'd say she took her clothes off voluntarily.'

'Liz found her briefs, Alex,' Murray said. 'So we'll be able to cross-check for semen as well as doing analysis on the other clothing.'

The pathologist dipped his head in acknowledgement, then turned back to Knox. 'Ed told you he found tyre tracks?'

'Yes,' Knox said. 'Looks like the killer ended her life somewhere within an hour's drive, and brought the body here.'

Turley nodded. 'Okay, I've done all I can do for the moment. I've just rang my assistants to pick up the body.' He turned back to Murray. 'You and Liz are finished at the locus, Ed?'

'Yeah,' Murray replied. 'We completed photography and videography before the Dalkeith boys came and tented the body. We'll go over the ground again once she's been moved.'

'You'll update me ASAP on the forensics?' Knox said. 'Particularly the tracks. If we can match them up it might give us an idea of the make of car.'

'I'll let you know as soon as, Jack,' Murray replied.

'Thanks,' Knox said. He turned to Turley. 'When do you reckon you'll finish the PM, Alex?'

Turley glanced at his watch. 'Late afternoon, somewhere around five. You'll stop by, rather than phone? There's someone I want you to meet.'

Knox was intrigued. 'Really?' he said. 'Who?'

A faint smile played around Turley's lips. 'Our new forensic pathologist, Lucinda Carmichael,' he said. 'She'll replace me when I retire at the end of the year.'

Knox was visibly taken aback. 'You're joking, surely?'

'Nearly sixty, Jack,' Turley said. 'Can't expect me to go on forever, now can you?'

'Oh, come now, Alex,' Knox replied with a twinkle in his eye. 'A man in as good fettle as you are? I don't see why not.'

* * *

Lowland Independent Television's Edinburgh Studio was located in Holyrood Road, a short distance from the Scottish Parliament. Senior reporter Jackie Lyon was seated at her desk in the newsroom, editing a programme called *Scotland in Focus*, due to be broadcast at 10.30 that evening.

The recording featured a meeting with the Cabinet Secretary for Justice, Alan Selkirk, whom she was interviewing regarding early prisoner release.

Lyon rewound the tape to the section she wanted, pressed *play*, and watched herself say: 'Your Conservative opposite number, Noel Addison, said in Parliament that the early prisoner release project is flawed. Two men freed under the scheme have already reoffended. One originally sentenced for housebreaking and, more seriously, the other a rapist. Doesn't that prove what Mr Addison said is true, Justice Minister – that the scheme isn't working?'

'No,' Selkirk said defensively. 'The prisoner release project has been in operation for over six months now, and as I said to Mr Addison in the chamber, some seven hundred other prisoners have been discharged, none of whom have reoffended. The two he cites constitute a *very* small percentage, well within projected estimates.'

'But one was convicted for rape,' Lyon said. 'Surely the member has a point?'

'If the man had attacked a woman, I'd agree,' Selkirk said. 'However that isn't the case. His offence was a breach of parole.'

Lyon changed tack. 'Okay,' she said, 'I'd like to move on to the subject of the heavy-handed behaviour of certain police officers. Two incidents, both in the last month: one involving an officer who hurt an elderly man at a football match in Glasgow, and another who struck a woman in Dumfries.'

Selkirk nodded. 'Officers from Police Scotland's Professional Standards Department are currently investigating both. First reports suggest the gentleman at Parkhead was accidently knocked down by an officer pursuing a man who assaulted another with a knife.

'The woman in Dumfries, a Mrs Sandra Yule, had been at a party. When neighbours complained about noise, police attended. Mrs Yule then became abusive and violent and had to be arrested. Police claim she struck a female officer who had no option but to subdue her with force.'

'Is it not a fact that Mrs Yule was struck by a baton, and had to have a gash on her forehead stitched at Dumfries Royal Infirmary?'

Selkirk shifted uncomfortably. 'Yes, I believe so. But like I say, both cases are still under investigation by Police Scotland's Professional Standards Department.'

At that moment the telephone on Lyon's desk rang. She paused the recording and picked up the handset. 'Hello... Lyon,' she said.

'Elena at reception with a call for you, Ms Lyon,' a voice said. 'A Mr Miles Read.'

'Can't say I know him,' Lyon said.

'Tells me he's a solicitor,' the receptionist replied. 'Says he'd like to speak in connection with something you're covering in this week's programme.'

'Really?' Lyon said, and glanced at the paused image of the Justice Secretary on her monitor. 'Put him through.'

There was a brief lull on the line and a voice said, 'Ms Lyon?'

'Yes, Mr Read,' she replied. 'What can I do for you?'

'I've just been looking at the television listings in today's *Scotsman*,' Read said. 'I gather you've conducted an interview with the Justice Secretary... on police brutality?'

'That'll be one of the items covered, yes. Why?'

'One of my clients, a Mr Edward Gilliland, is in an ICU unit at Edinburgh Royal Infirmary as a result of an assault by an officer from Gayfield Square Police Station. I thought the case might be of interest.'

'It might,' Lyon said. 'Where did this happen, and when?'

'At Pik-Pak Electrical and Telephonic Supplies, Newhaven Road,' Read said. 'Last Saturday.'

'Go on.'

'Mr Gilliland is charged with the theft of a mobile phone, but the degree of force used in detaining him was excessive. Detective Sergeant William Fulton, the arresting officer, is six foot tall and heavily built. His tackle brought Gilliland to the floor, where all seventeen stone of him landed on my client, a slight man in his late teens.'

'What are the nature of Mr Gilliland's injuries?'

'Fulton's tackle caused him to connect with the edge of a pallet. He broke a middle rib and suffered a punctured lung.'

'Gilliland admitted the theft?'

'No, unfit to plead. He was taken directly from the store to the Royal Infirmary. I'm being retained by his mother.'

'She's bringing the charge?'

'Yes.'

'Any evidence to back it up?'

'She received a phone call from a Pik-Pak employee, who witnessed the arrest. She claims Fulton's actions were heavy-handed.'

'Who's the witness?'

'She prefers to remain anonymous.'

'What was the police response?'

'As you'd expect, they won't admit to anything. However, they've initiated an investigation.'

'You told them Gilliland's mother was bringing a charge?'

'Yes,' Read replied. 'I spoke to Chief Superintendent Ian Ross at their Gartcosh HQ. He told me their Professional Standards Department would investigate.'

'Mm-hmm, Professional Standards,' Lyon said. 'They must be taking it seriously.' A pause, then, 'Okay, Mr Read, thanks for bringing this to my attention. Might be something I can use. I'll make a couple of phone calls and get back to you.'

'Of course you appreciate that this is off the record?'

'Naturally, Mr Read,' Lyon said. 'My sources always retain their anonymity.'

Chapter Six

'So our killer's the guy who confessed to the priest?' Fulton was saying. It was a little after 2pm and the detectives were discussing the discovery of the girl at Pathhead. 'The clothes check out?' he added. 'It's definitely Laura Winter?'

'He probably is,' Knox said. 'And, yes, they're hers.'

'She died the way he said?'

'Uh-huh,' Knox replied. 'Strangulation.'

He went to a whiteboard, wrote 'THE CONFESSOR', and turned to the others. 'Okay, let's go over what we know: male, late twenties, early thirties. Well spoken. Has a car, but was probably on foot when he visited St Bridget's. Any ideas?'

'He lives in Leith?' Hathaway ventured.

Knox nodded and scrawled 'LOCAL' on the board. 'Very likely. I've a hunch he's familiar with the area, saw the priest on a whim. Anybody else?'

'Wondering how he met the girl, boss,' Fulton said. 'The B&B woman said Laura didn't know anyone. She only arrived on Wednesday.'

'True,' Knox replied. 'Arlene checked airline schedules on our way back from Pathhead. Only one flight from Toronto, on which she travelled alone. Arrived at 15.05. We asked airport police to check CCTV records. They confirm no one met her.'

'Mrs Carter said the Scottish Tourist Board at the Waverley rang about accommodation?' Hathaway asked.

'Yes,' McCann said. 'Around 4pm, an hour before she arrived at Links Place.'

'Fits,' Hathaway said. 'Roughly forty minutes from the airport. Likely she took a tram.'

'Doesn't tell us how she ran into her killer,' Fulton said. He turned to Knox. 'It's possible he gave her a lift? Attempted rape?'

'No,' Knox said. 'She knew her killer; went willingly. Turley says her clothes were removed voluntarily.'

'What about the carpet salesman, Peabody?' McCann said.

Knox dipped his head in agreement. 'Yeah, she might've mentioned something. Our only hope until we see forensics.' He fished in his pocket, found the card, and handed it to Hathaway. 'Give him a ring, Mark. Probably back in Leeds now, but no matter. See what he says.'

The DCI's door opened at that moment and Warburton beckoned to Knox. 'Jack,' he said. 'Can I see you a moment?' Then to Fulton, he added, 'You'd better come too, Bill.'

Warburton waved to a couple of chairs as they entered and addressed Knox, 'Any leads yet?'

'No, sir,' Knox replied. 'McCann and I interviewed the owners of the guest house but didn't pick up on anything significant. A carpet company rep spoke to her there, which we're currently following up. Tyre tracks at the locus might tell us the make of car the killer drove. We're hoping, too, for DNA and other evidence from her clothes.'

Warburton nodded. 'Good, keep me up to speed.' A pause. 'However, that's not the only reason I've called you in.' He gestured to a phone on his desk. 'I've just taken a call from Chief Superintendent Ian Ross – the officer who liaises with the Justice Secretary on police matters.' Warburton cleared his throat, glanced at Fulton, and continued, 'It's to do with Gilliland, Bill.'

'Not much more I can add to what I told DCI Simmonds and DI Collins, sir,' Fulton said.

'I know. DCI Simmonds told me they're going to speak to a couple of employees who weren't at the warehouse this morning.'

'Yes, sir,' Fulton said. 'He explained.'

The chief shook his head. 'We've another problem. The media's got hold of it – Jackie Lyon at Lowland Independent Television.'

Fulton had a sharp intake of breath. 'Jesus,' he said. 'Torquemada in drawers.' Then, suddenly conscious of who he was talking to, added, 'Sorry, sir.'

Warburton gave a thin smile. 'It's okay, Bill. Not a bad description.'

'Lyon,' Knox said. 'She's going public – even though Complaints haven't concluded their investigation?'

'It would seem so,' Warburton said. 'Just happens that *Scotland in Focus* is featuring an interview with the Justice Minister this week. One of the topics is excessive use of force when apprehending miscreants – the rookie PC in Dumfries, the old chap hurt in the fracas at Parkhead.

Ross tells me the interview with Selkirk is in the can, but Lyon wants to add a piece on Gilliland.'

'No prizes for guessing who told her,' Knox said.

'No,' Warburton agreed. 'The brief; seeking to bias opinion towards his client.'

'And CS Ross sanctioned it?' Knox said.

Warburton shrugged. 'It's PR,' he replied. 'Like I say, he's liaison officer with Holyrood.'

'The interview with Lyon?' Knox said. 'He wants you to do it?'

'I'm afraid so,' Warburton said.

'Not for the fainthearted, sir,' Knox said. 'If you don't mind me saying.'

'I don't, Jack. And I know what she's like. Crossed swords a couple of years ago, remember?'

'I do,' Knox said. 'When a similar charge was brought against me after the arrest of David McIntyre in the Cowgate.' Knox shook his head. 'Look, sir, there's no need for you to see her alone. I'm Bill's supervising officer: let me take the interview with you.'

Warburton studied Knox for a moment. 'Would you?' he said.

'There isn't anything in the rulebook to say that we can't,' Knox said.

The DCI brightened a little. 'No,' he replied. 'No, there isn't. Thanks, Jack; it would make it a damn sight less intimidating.'

'What time are you seeing her?'

'CS Ross arranged the interview for 6.15pm, at LIT's Holyrood Road studios.'

'Fine,' Knox said. 'I'm meeting Alex Turley at the Cowgate at 5pm about Laura Winter's PM. I'll meet you there afterwards.'

* * *

He awoke suddenly, soaked in sweat. The nightmare he'd experienced over the last few nights had occurred again.

A coffin in a dark empty room: intense rumbling thunder and prolonged flashes of lightning. His eyes drawn like a magnet at every coruscation.

The coffin, the only item visible, had been placed on trestles. There was a further flash, and screws began to unwind. Threaded pieces of metal popped free and fell to the floor.

The room lapsed into darkness as the lightning ceased, then he heard the lid slide. The long shadow on the trestles, now barely visible, continued to fix his gaze.

There was a final burst of light, and he saw his mother rise from within. The eyes in her waxen face looked directly into his, her skeletal arm reaching out, bony finger extended. Then her voice; strident, otherworldly, echoed across the room.

'See what evil's brought you,' she said, adding, 'You've become possessed. Your soul's become possessed…'

He jumped out of bed and rushed to the bathroom, ran the cold tap and splashed his face. As he grabbed a towel and began drying, his heart rate returned to normal, and moments later his thoughts went back to the confession.

Seeing the Yank, he realised, had been a mistake.

The priest he'd visited when his mother died had been kind and solicitous – in contrast to the one at St Bridget's, who'd been aloof and intractable.

He'd been in two minds when the verger asked him to wait. Particularly after he heard one of the women whisper: "The priest's on an inter-church exchange from St Benedict's in Boston".

He went ahead, though, hoping Murphy would be receptive to his plea for exorcism. But no, the pious son of a bitch implied he needed psychiatric help instead: "I think it's possible you're ill, my son, and I suggest you confess."

Aye, right.

He went to the kitchen, switched on the percolator, the nightmare still vivid in his mind. "See what evil's brought you," his mother said, echoing a sentiment she'd spoken in life.

She was talking about the rape… the rape he hadn't committed.

His conviction lay at the centre of a rift between them: a rift that lasted until her death.

It took place soon after his sixteenth birthday. The girl, Amanda, lived a couple of streets away and was two years younger. One of a group of kids who hung around the area where they lived.

She was mature for her years, both physically and in manner.

He knew she'd a crush as every time their paths crossed, she went out of her way to say hello. At first he took no notice, other than to say hello in return. But soon her infatuation became ever more apparent. On the day it took place he was on his way to the shops when she stopped on her bicycle.

'Hi, Raymond,' she said.

He turned to face her, and for the first time he paid attention. Her blouse was open; the top of her firm, rounded breasts clearly visible. 'Hi,' he replied.

She leaned back in the saddle, hitching up her skirt and flashing her underwear. 'I'm going to Figgate Park this afternoon,' she said. 'Want to meet up?'

He did, of course, and soon after they met he went with her into a clump of bushes and had sex.

She'd given him an invitation, and he'd taken advantage. What he didn't expect was that police would come calling and he'd be charged with rape.

The little cow had seduced him, then ran to her parents, claiming he forced himself on her.

The charge was a disaster for his mother.

He was an only child, whose father had died when he was three, and she had brought him up on her own. A member of the local Women's Institute, she was a dignified woman who believed herself a paragon of respectability. Naturally, she was mortified her son had taken advantage of an underage girl.

He was taken before a juvenile panel, who judged him guilty. In light of his mother's good standing, however, he was spared detention in a young offender's institution and given one hundred hours of community service.

Not that this mattered to anyone in his mother's circle. Her membership of the WI was revoked and she became a social pariah, shunned by friends and neighbours alike. This 'sending to Coventry' became so hard to bear that she moved to another part of town.

Other than an initial admonishment, she never spoke on the subject. Yet the incident drove a wedge between them that lasted until she died at the age of forty-seven.

He joined the Royal Logistics Corps a year after the hearing. Partly because the idea of adventure appealed, but mainly because he wanted to get away. His mother hadn't objected: glad, perhaps, that he was going.

Army training involved learning to drive heavy vehicles, and soon after completion he was posted to Belize, where he was serving when news came that she was suffering with cancer. He was allowed compassionate leave, and arrived back just days before she died.

In hospital his mother had been unconscious, rallying only for a few minutes. She gazed into his eyes and said weakly, 'Why did you do it, Raymond?'

There was no point repeating it hadn't been rape, that Amanda had participated willingly. All he could think of to say was, 'I'm sorry, Mum.'

Her eyes closed, and she drifted into a coma from which she never awoke.

After her funeral he served a further six years, returning to civilian life to become a long-distance truck driver.

Two years of tramping motorways allowed little social life, however, and he came back to Edinburgh, where a mate recommended private hire.

He had placed his mother's house with a property agency when she died, but by then the lease had ended, and he was able to move back in.

He showered and shaved, had breakfast and got dressed, then went to the garage and backed out his car. He took a mobile from the glove compartment, clicked on an app marked "2Ucab", and signed in.

Moments later there was a loud *ping* and he glanced at the screen. The iPhone displayed a section of the city between Waverley Station, highlighted in red, and Milton Road East, above which was captioned: "Pick up (C. Mullen) at 11.14, 4.4 miles, £12.80. Tap to accept".

He tapped and the screen flashed, "Hire accepted".

The traffic was light and it took just twelve minutes to cover the short distance from his home to the pick-up point at Waverley Station.

A small knot of people were waiting at the rank, among which was a girl in her twenties, who was holding a case. She watched him approach, pointed to his nearside window, and motioned for him to unwind. He did so and she said, '2Ucabs?'

'Yes, Ms Mullen?' he asked.

'Uh-huh.' She replied. 'For the Brunstane Hotel?'

'That's right,' he said, smiling. 'Wait a sec, I'll put your case in the boot.'

Chapter Seven

Knox's call on the intercom at the Cowgate Mortuary was answered by a woman whose voice he didn't recognise. 'Hello?' she said.

'DI Knox to see Alex Turley,' he replied.

'Just a moment.' There was a brief pause, and Knox heard the buzzer sound again, accompanied by a click of the lock. He pushed the door and entered a short corridor, where he was met by an attractive woman in her early thirties.

She had high cheekbones and an oval face, framed by ash-blonde shoulder-length hair. She smiled and extended her hand. 'Lucinda Carmichael,' she said. 'But I prefer Lucy.'

Knox returned her smile and shook her hand. 'Lucy,' he said. 'You're the new pathologist Alex was telling me about?'

She gave a little laugh which brought a twinkle to her blue-grey eyes. 'Not all that new,' she said. 'But, yes, I'm his assistant.' She waved to a door at the end of the passageway. 'He's in the PM room, Detective Inspector.'

Knox grinned. 'I prefer Jack,' he said, 'and it's nice to meet you.'

'Nice to meet you, too,' Carmichael said.

Knox nodded to the examination room. 'Laura Winter,' he said. 'The autopsy's done?'

'Almost,' she replied. 'I gave Alex a hand earlier and left him to finish up. I was in the office finalising some analysis reports.' She pointed to coveralls on hooks on the wall at her back. 'We'd better gown up before we go in.'

A few moments later they stood before a fixed metal table in the centre of the examination room, on which the body of Laura Winter lay prone, a white plastic sheet drawn to her ankles. Turley stood at the head, Carmichael and Knox alongside.

'Further examination confirmed my analysis at the scene,' the pathologist said. 'All the indications are that the killer exerted pressure in excess of 35 pounds, cutting off her airway. The fact that the hyoid bone's fractured confirms this.'

'Any touch-DNA on her neck?' Knox asked.

'No,' Turley said. 'She's been out in the elements for more than a week, Jack. Exposure and decomposition rule that out.'

'You confirmed your estimate, though,' Knox said. 'She'd been at Pathhead for around ten days?'

Carmichael indicated an I-shaped incision running from the neck to the pubic area, which had recently been sutured. 'I took specimens from her spleen, liver and heart, and analysed the bacterial content of each. These tests track microbiome changes, pinpointing the time elapsed since death. They verify she died in the early hours of Saturday, 14 March.'

Knox dipped his head in acknowledgement, and Turley said, 'Have the results of the tyre prints come through, Jack? Anything on her clothes?'

'Not yet,' Knox replied. 'Murray and Beattie are still with forensics at Howdenhall. They've promised to get in touch the moment they find anything.'

'Aye,' Turley said. 'These things take time.' He moved away from the table and nodded towards the door. 'You'll have a coffee before you go?'

Knox checked his watch and saw it was 5.15pm. 'Meeting my boss at six,' he said. 'Only a short drive, though: LIT Studios in Holyrood Road. We're doing an interview.'

'Plenty of time,' Turley said. 'Come through and I'll switch on the coffee maker. Won't take long.'

A few minutes later they were seated in his office with three steaming cups on the table before them. 'So, Jack,' he said, 'what do you think of my new assistant?'

Knox glanced at Carmichael, who rolled her eyes. 'Stop it, Alex,' she said. 'You'll embarrass the man.'

'A legitimate question,' Turley said. 'Since it won't be long till my retirement and you'll be seeing a lot of each other.'

'Well, naturally, I'll miss you, Alex,' Knox said, then winked at Carmichael and added, 'but I'm sure we'll get along just fine.' He took a swallow of coffee, glanced at Carmichael, and asked, 'You live in the city?'

'I'm in the process of moving,' she said. 'From Dundee. I was with Central Division's forensic lab there.'

'You found a place?' Knox asked.

Carmichael took a sip of her coffee and returned the cup to the table. 'Yes,' she said. 'I'm currently in the process of concluding missives on a flat in Ratcliffe Terrace.'

'Really?' Knox said. 'Then we'll be neighbours. Well, almost. I live half a mile away, East Parkside.'

Carmichael shook her head. 'I'm afraid I don't know the city that well.'

'Well there you are,' Turley said with a sly smile. 'Why don't you do the neighbourly thing, Jack, and show her around?'

Carmichael gave Turley an embarrassed look. 'Really, Alex,' she said. 'Behave yourself.'

Turley feigned a hurt expression and was silent for a moment, then said, 'Your rendezvous with DCI Warburton at LIT, Jack,' he said. 'Pardon my nose, but the interview – it's to do with the case?'

'No, something else,' Knox said. 'Unnecessary force has been alleged in an arrest made by one of my officers, which DCI Warburton and I intend to refute.'

Turley looked surprised. 'Really,' he said. 'Which officer?'

'DS Bill Fulton,' Knox said. 'He collared a thief at an electrical store in Newhaven Road on Saturday. A young lad stole a mobile phone, attempted to flee, and Bill tripped him up. He suffered a broken rib, which punctured a lung and was taken to hospital and admitted to ICU.'

'His solicitor's made the charge formal?' Turley asked.

'Yeah,' Knox replied. 'And Complaints are involved.'

'They've talked to Bill?'

'Yeah, earlier today.'

'How's it looking?'

'All down to witnesses,' Knox said. 'The thief – a guy called Edward Gilliland – came into contact with a pallet. Bill says it happened when he tripped. Miles Read, the solicitor, claims it took place afterwards. According to him, Bill deliberately pushed Gilliland when he put on the handcuffs. The only witness spoken to so far isn't sure, as it happened so fast. Two other witnesses were off duty when the Complaints officers called.'

Turley pursed his lips. 'Your meeting,' he said. 'Let me guess – it's with Jackie Lyon?'

'Yeah,' Knox replied. 'Her *Scotland in Focus* programme going out later tonight features an interview with the Justice Secretary. No prizes for guessing the subject.'

'It's a programme I don't often watch,' Carmichael said. 'But she seems a very formidable lady.'

Knox gave a rueful nod. 'That's putting it mildly.'

'Wasn't Warburton interviewed by her a couple of years ago?' Turley asked. 'When a similar thing happened to you?'

'Aye,' Knox said. 'A charge later thrown out by the Procurator Fiscal. The DCI found the interview *very* uncomfortable.'

'Which is why you'll be with him this time?' Carmichael asked.

Knox smiled. 'Exactly,' he said, and added, 'I offered, thought it might deflect any heat. He accepted.'

Turley motioned towards Carmichael and grinned. 'Proof that Lucy's forensic abilities aren't confined to the lab.' There was a brief pause and he went on, 'Read would have brought the case to Lyon's attention?'

'I think so,' Knox said. 'Apparently she'd already done an interview with Alan Selkirk on the subject. Gilliland's solicitor must have found out about it and…' Knox shrugged and let it hang.

'And realised fate had just dropped a gift horse into his lap,' Turley said. 'Well, Jack, I wish you all the best. You'll need all your wits about you with Lyon.'

Knox gave him a sardonic look. 'Tune in at 10.30 tonight and see if I succeed.'

'Naturally, I'll make a point of watching.' Turley turned to Carmichael and added, 'You, Lucy?'

'Of course,' she said and smiled at Knox. 'And I'm sure you'll be fine.'

* * *

A few minutes later Knox was back in his car. He placed his iPhone on the dash, keyed in a number, and pressed *call*. After a couple of rings he heard a familiar voice: 'Boss?'

'Hi, Bill,' Knox said. 'I'm at the Cowgate, about to head down to LIT studios to meet the chief. Did Mark have any luck in locating Peabody?'

'Eventually,' Fulton said. 'The card gave his office number. A receptionist there gave out his mobile. Mark rang it and got through to him.'

'And?'

'Aye, he and Laura Winter appear to have had a lengthy chinwag. She told him she'd discovered her great-grandfather on her mother's side came from Mull and was looking forward to visiting the island. Apparently she'd been in contact with an online ancestry group here in Edinburgh. She informed Peabody she'd a meeting on Friday, 13 March with a genealogist.'

'The day she went missing?'

'Uh-huh,' Fulton said.

'Mm-hmm,' Knox said. 'Pity we didn't find her backpack. A mobile phone or tablet would've given us access to her e-mails.'

'Mark and I discussed that,' Fulton said. 'He went online; checked genealogy groups in Edinburgh. Only four, it seems. Sent an e-mail to the administrator of each, asking if Laura was a member. That was just over an hour ago. Haven't heard anything yet.'

'Did Peabody say if she was meeting anyone else?'

'No, only the genealogist.'

'Well, it's a start,' Knox said. 'You contacted Ontario Police?'

'Aye,' Fulton replied. 'They'll break the news to Laura's mother. I also asked if they'd find out her daughter's e-mail address and internet service provider, see if anything can be traced that way.'

'Good idea, Bill,' Knox said and checked his watch. 'Okay, it's almost six. I reckon you, Mark and Arlene can call it a day.'

'Mr Turley,' Fulton said. 'He confirmed cause of death?'

'Aye,' Knox said. 'And the fact that Laura had been taken to Pathhead in the early hours of the fourteenth.'

A long silence followed, then Fulton said, 'You're on your way to see Lyon now?'

'Yes. Meeting the chief at six. Interview's scheduled for quarter past.'

When Fulton said nothing, Knox added, 'Nothing to worry about, Bill. This is Gilliland's solicitor's attempt to put on pressure. When I was in the firing line a couple of years ago, it was you who told me "Facts are chiels that winna ding," remember? The truth will out, in other words. Complaints will likely have spoken to other witnesses who'll have vouched for what happened. Lyon's interview is a damp squib; it'll fizzle out, believe me.'

'You're probably right, boss.' Fulton said. 'DCI Collins did say it would be a day or two before they let me have the verdict.'

'There you go,' Knox said brightly. 'Lyon is simply playing to the gallery.'

* * *

Warburton was pacing nervously beside his car when Knox pulled into Lowland Independent Television's parking area. He exited the Passat, activated the central locking, and went over to his boss. 'Waiting long, sir?' he said.

'Only five minutes,' Warburton replied, then shivered and added gloomily, 'felt more like fifty.'

Knox checked his watch. 'Only just six, sir.' They're bound to have a coffee machine. I'll get us some before we head into the studio.'

Moments later he and the DCI stood in the reception area, where they were met by a strawberry-haired girl in her early twenties who flashed them a broad smile. 'You're DCI Warburton?' she said.

'Yes,' Warburton replied, and waved towards Knox. 'And this is Detective Inspector Knox, DS Fulton's team leader. He'll be taking the interview with me. I did explain when I phoned ahead.'

'Yes, sir, it was me you spoke to – Elena Harper. I'm Ms Lyon's PA. I mentioned it to her, she told me she was okay with it.'

'Wee bit cold out there,' Knox said, motioning towards the entrance. 'Would it be possible for us to have a coffee?'

'Of course,' Harper said, nodding to a table surrounded by leather chairs. 'Have a seat and I'll bring some.' She checked her watch. 'Plenty of time; we've twenty-five minutes before recording.'

Chapter Eight

A light at the front of a camera trained on Lyon blinked red, and she glanced up from her desk and looked into the lens. 'That was Justice Minister Alan Selkirk speaking to me earlier today,' she said. 'We're staying with the subject of force used in police arrests, and to discuss this with me are two officers from Gayfield Police Station here in Edinburgh; Detective Chief Inspector Ronald Warburton, and Detective Inspector Jack Knox.'

She turned to face them and said, 'Good evening, gentlemen. Thanks for coming in to speak to me.'

Warburton and Knox gave acknowledging nods, but said nothing.

'Viewers have just listened to Alan Selkirk and I discussed two cases where it is claimed members of the public were injured through excessive use of force,' Lyon said. 'One in Glasgow and the other in Dumfries.' She paused and added, 'Now we discover that over the weekend a man was taken to hospital in Edinburgh with a life-threatening injury sustained due to the manner of his arrest.'

Knox glanced at a monitor alongside the camera and saw the picture cut from Lyon to Warburton, who'd begun to perspire.

'DCI Warburton,' Lyon continued, 'I believe the officer involved in the arrest is one of your men, based at Gayfield Square Police Station?'

Warburton cleared his throat. 'Yes,' he replied, his voice croaking slightly. 'The detective who made the arrest is one of my officers.'

Lyon consulted her notes. 'And the man arrested, a Mr Edward Gilliland, is currently in intensive care at Edinburgh Royal Infirmary. He sustained a broken rib, which unfortunately penetrated a lung, causing it to collapse. Would you care to comment on how that happened?'

'Perhaps I can answer,' Knox said. He glanced at the monitor to confirm the picture had switched from Warburton to himself, and continued, 'It was last Saturday, 21 March, and the officer was off duty. He happened to be in the store where the incident occurred.'

'This man is part of your team, Detective Inspector?' Lyon said.

'Yes.'

'Please, go on.'

'Mr Gilliland broke a mobile from a cord tethering it to its display case and placed it in a holdall. The theft was witnessed by a security guard, who asked him to open the holdall. Gilliland refused, and there was a commotion. My officer observed this, showed Gilliland his warrant card, and told him to comply. The man made a run for it and my officer tripped him up. Gilliland struck a pallet when he fell.'

'Really, Detective Inspector?' Lyon said. 'Isn't it true your officer conducted a forceful arrest, thrusting Mr Gilliland into the pallet? Didn't that cause the injury?'

'No, my officer insists it was a result of the fall.'

'The security guard,' Lyon said, 'he witnessed the incident?'

'Yes.'

'And yet when I contacted the store – Pik-Pak in Newhaven Road – the guard told me he was unable to say for sure exactly how Mr Gilliland came by his injury.'

'Apparently he didn't have a clear view from where he was standing,' Knox said. 'It happened very fast.'

'Yes,' Lyon said. 'I spoke to the guard in question, and that's exactly what he told me: it happened fast.' She paused for effect. 'Fact is, there's nothing to corroborate your officer's version of events at all, is there, Detective Inspector?'

'Officers from our Professional Standards Department are currently investigating the incident,' Warburton said, regaining his composure. 'And it appears there was more than one witness. The outcome of their inquiries will be released later this week.'

'Ah, I see, Detective Chief Inspector,' Lyon said. 'Your Professional Standards Department; am I correct in thinking they're asked to investigate if a charge of excessive force has been made?'

Warburton nodded. 'That's correct, yes.'

'The officer has been interviewed?'

'Yes.'

'Would I also be correct in the assumption that a complaint has in fact been made by Mr Gilliland's solicitor, Mr Miles Read?'

Knox shot Lyon a cynical look that said: *As if you didn't know.*

Warburton cleared his throat again and answered her question. 'Yes,' he said. 'It has.'

'Yet the officer remains on duty?'

'Only in an administrative capacity,' Warburton said.

'You mean he's not allowed to take part in any active investigation?'

'Not outside our offices, no.'

'A form of suspension, in other words?'

Warburton shook his head. 'No, the officer hasn't been suspended. It's procedure in cases such as this.'

'So you think it's possible there's a case to answer – the officer may indeed be guilty?'

Once again Warburton appeared uncomfortable. He ran a finger under his collar, and a sheen of sweat was visible on his forehead.

Knox cut in. 'No, it doesn't,' he said sharply. 'It's as DCI Warburton says – being confined to administrative duties is part of operational procedure. Suspension is enacted only when a charge is proven.'

Lyon locked eyes with Knox. 'So,' she said, 'just to recap, Detective Inspector, your Professional Standards Department is in the process of interviewing witnesses, but the only one so far is unclear what happened? And their findings will be made public later this week, meanwhile the officer who made the arrest is still on duty. Is that a fair summary?'

'As DCI Warburton said,' Knox replied, 'the officer *is* on duty, but in an administrative role.'

The camera close-focussed on Lyon and she gave a look of triumph. 'Thank you. And while we await Police Scotland's verdict, Mr Gilliland lies seriously injured in an intensive care unit at Edinburgh Royal Infirmary.'

The *Scotland in Focus* signature music began and she added, 'Okay, that's all for tonight and thanks for watching. Tune in again on Friday when we'll update you on the latest on this case and others covered in tonight's edition. My thanks in the meantime to Justice Minister

Alan Selkirk, Detective Chief Inspector Ronald Warburton, and Detective Inspector Jack Knox for their participation.' She shuffled her papers and smiled into the lens. 'Goodnight.'

* * *

'What a beautiful part of the city,' Cassandra Mullen was saying. Five minutes had passed since he'd picked her up at the Waverley, and they were driving through Holyrood Park. 'I didn't realise there was such a huge area of greenery in the centre of town.'

'Most people don't,' he said. 'This is Queen's Drive, part of Holyrood Park. It connects with London Road, gives access to the eastern part of town.'

A moment later they approached a long lake, where a group of people were feeding ducks waddling near the water's edge. 'Oh,' she said. 'There's even a duck pond.'

He smiled. 'St Margaret's Loch,' he said, slowing to allow her a better view. 'Is this your first time in Edinburgh?'

'No,' she said, 'second. Last time I stayed near the airport. The Post House Hotel.'

He gave a nod of understanding. 'Corstorphine.'

'Yes,' Mullen agreed. 'I was here for a couple of days then, too. Didn't get a chance to do much sightseeing.'

'You're here on business?'

Mullen inclined her head. 'Yes. With a company called Leonis, a cosmetics manufacturer. I see buyers at some of the bigger department stores, try to get them to increase their orders.'

'And you're successful?'

She grinned. 'More often than not.'

He smiled back at her. 'I'd have guessed you were.' He paused, and added, 'Successful, I mean.'

Mullen gave him an appraising look. He was square-jawed and handsome, with dark curly hair, penetrating blue eyes and a captivating smile.

'Thank you,' she said.

'I've been trying to place your accent,' he said. 'I'd have said somewhere in the Midlands, but I'm not sure.'

'West Country – Poole in Dorset. I've been in London for more than four years, though. I'm sure living there has taken off the rougher edges.'

He stopped at a set of traffic lights at that moment and looked directly into her eyes. 'Sorry,' he said. 'I didn't intend to be rude. You have a very pleasant voice.'

'You must hear all kinds of accents in your business,' she replied.

'Yes – more so in summer and during the Festival.'

'You've been with 2Ucabs long?'

'Nearly three years,' he replied, 'I was a long-distance lorry driver before that.'

'Oh,' she said. 'Not much of a life for a man with a family.'

'No family,' he said with a shrug. 'I'm not married.'

They drove in silence for a couple of minutes, then he said, 'Your meetings with buyers, you're taking any later today?'

She shook her head. 'Not today, no. I'll spend the rest of the day going over my presentations. I'll also be checking e-mails, as I expect my boss to update me on a new line of perfume we're introducing. I'll be seeing buyers tomorrow.'

He dipped his head in acknowledgement. 'The reason I asked was in case you needed transport back into town. I'd be only too happy to give you a special rate.'

'That's kind of you,' she said. 'But no, I'm not planning to go out until later.'

He slowed the car and signalled right, turned into the driveway of the Brunstane Hotel, and stopped. 'I'll get your case from the boot,' he said. After a moment's hesitation, he turned to face her and added, 'I hope you don't think it forward, but would you like to go out with me? You mentioned you weren't able to do much sightseeing last time you were here. It'd be my pleasure to show you around.'

She looked at him coquettishly. 'You're asking for a date?'

'Yes,' he said. 'Yes, I am.'

She held his gaze for a long moment. 'Okay,' she said.

'Great,' he said, beaming. 'Would six o'clock be okay?'

'Six o'clock would be just fine.'

'Great,' he repeated and stuck out his hand. 'I'm Raymond, by the way.'

She shook it, and replied, 'Nice to meet you, Raymond.' She paused, and added, 'I'm Cassie.'

* * *

'That look you gave Lyon when she mentioned Gilliland's brief was priceless,' McCann was saying. It was Tuesday morning and Knox's team were discussing the television interview of the previous evening.

'Aye, boss, you more than held your own,' Fulton agreed. 'Still, she did everything she could to keep up the negative agenda. Guilty till proved innocent, eh?'

'It's the witness statements that matter,' Knox said, nodding towards Warburton's office. 'The chief tipped me the wink earlier – Gartcosh's been on the line. DCI Collins and DI Simmonds spoke to the Pik-Pak employees late yesterday. Apparently they've concluded the interviews.'

'Was Collins able to give him the verdict?' Fulton said earnestly.

'Not yet, Bill. He told me they're still picking over the men's statements. We'll know either tomorrow or Thursday.'

Fulton shook his head dolefully. 'And in the meantime I'm stuck here.'

Knox grinned. 'Where you'll be every bit as effective as anywhere else.'

Fulton gave a shrug. 'I suppose. By the way, I meant to say that we've had a reply to our e-mails to the ancestry groups. One called Caledonian Heritage.'

'The person Laura Winter corresponded with?'

Fulton nodded towards Hathaway. 'I think so. It came in on Mark's computer.'

'Yes, boss,' Hathaway said. 'Sent at 11.23pm last night.' Hathaway opened his e-mail folder and double-clicked on a message. 'A guy called George Middleton. Says Ms Winter was in regular contact with him until Wednesday, 11 March. They met on Friday thirteenth, in the afternoon.'

'Where?' Knox asked.

Hathaway studied the screen for a moment and said, 'Aye, here we are. He says he had a drink with her on the High Street. Just after 2pm.'

'Does he give his phone number?' Knox asked.

Hathaway glanced back at the screen. 'Aye, boss. We've got it.'

'Good,' Knox said. 'Give him a ring, will you, Mark? See if we can interview him this morning.'

'Boss.'

'Another thing I forgot to mention,' Fulton said. 'The RCMP called just before we left last night. They broke the news to Ms Winter's mother yesterday. Told us she'd arrive on the afternoon flight.'

'What time does it get in?' Knox asked.

'I checked,' McCann said. '4.36pm.'

'You arranged for someone to meet her?'

'Yes,' McCann replied. 'I spoke to Inspector Cox, grief counsellor at our Public Liaison office, they'll arrange to meet her at the airport and take her to Cowgate Mortuary. I asked the Liaison Office to keep us informed. Said we'd want to speak to her.'

'Good,' Knox said. 'I'll make sure I'm there when she arrives.'

At that moment DI Murray entered the office and joined the others. 'Morning, Jack; morning, all,' he said.

The detectives returned his greeting, and Knox asked, 'Any news on forensics, Ed?'

Murray placed an A4 folder on a nearby desk and said, 'Yes and no.' He took out a photograph and showed it to Knox. 'This is a print of a cast of the tyres on the track near where Laura Winter's body was found. All four are Michelin 195/65 R15. Size 91V.'

'Does that give us an indication of the car's make?' Knox asked.

'Yes,' Murray replied. 'We're pretty sure they're the original tyres fitted to a Toyota Prius. Minimal tread wear suggests a fairly new vehicle.'

'What about forensics from her clothes, sir?' McCann said. 'Any DNA?'

'DS Beattie's still at Howdenhall, analysing the results,' Murray replied. 'So far it appears negative on her coat, jeans and other items. We're not sure about the briefs, though. Liz thinks she'll be able to tell for sure later today.' Murray picked up the folder then and nodded towards Warburton's office. 'I'd better update the chief before I go.'

Knox inclined his head in acknowledgement. 'Okay, Ed,' he said. 'Thanks for the heads-up re the tyres; give me a ring if Liz finds anything else.'

As Murray headed for the DCI's office, Hathaway put down the telephone and handed Knox a note. 'Just spoke to Middleton, boss. He's a sous-chef at Sea Fare restaurant at Shore, Leith. He'll be there all day; finishes at six.'

'Right,' Knox said, nodding towards McCann. 'Arlene and I will head down and speak to him.' Then to Fulton, he said, 'Bill, you and Mark check Toyota dealerships in the Edinburgh area. Quote the tyre specs and see if it lets us narrow it down any – different models and buyers, that sort of thing; you might be able to work up a list. Also check with the DVLA to see how many Priuses were registered.'

'Righto, boss,' Fulton said.

Chapter Nine

'Laura Winter first contacted Caledonian Heritage in November last year,' George Middleton was saying. 'She had a copy of her great-grandfather's birth certificate and he was born in Glasgow.'

Knox and McCann were seated in a small pantry at the rear of the Sea Fare restaurant's kitchen and Middleton, a rotund man in his late forties, had a laptop open on a desk in front of him.

'Her post to our group said she was coming to Scotland in March this year,' he went on, 'asked if anyone could advise on how to trace further back. I accessed *Scotland's People* website to check and responded.'

'You were able to help her?' McCann asked.

'Of course. I entered her great-granddad's details in *Scotland's People*, which flagged up church records for Mull.' Middleton leaned forward, peered at the laptop, and traced a finger across the screen. 'Here we are: Calum Mackinnon, born 17 April, 1897 in Balmeanach.'

'Yet her grandfather came from Glasgow?' Knox asked.

Middleton nodded. 'Not uncommon. A lot of folk from the Scottish islands headed for the city in the third quarter of the nineteenth century. Plenty of jobs in the shipbuilding industry, which was enjoying a boom. Laura's great-grandfather went there too. He became a welder.'

'You forwarded this information to her in Canada?'

'Yes, as a PDF. She wrote back and said when she came to Scotland she would like to meet up and buy me a drink by way of thanks.'

'The officer you talked to this morning told us you met her on Friday, 13 March?'

'Aye, I did,' Middleton said, then gave Knox a quizzical look and added, 'look, your lad didn't say what was going on – Ms Winter's gone missing?'

Knox and McCann exchanged glances, then Knox said, 'I'm sorry to have to tell you, but I'm afraid she's been murdered. Her body was found on the outskirts of Edinburgh yesterday morning.'

Middleton's face blanched. 'Oh, jeez, no,' he said. A few moments passed, then he added, 'who in the name of God would do that?'

'Exactly what we intend finding out,' Knox said. 'Your e-mail said you met her that Friday?'

Middleton nodded. 'Yes, The Filling Station pub in the High Street, just after two.'

'How was the meeting arranged?' Knox asked.

'She phoned after she arrived on Wednesday, 11 March, told me she'd booked into a guest house in Leith. Arranged to meet up on Friday.'

'Was this the first time you'd spoken?' Knox said. 'Your previous communications had been by e-mail?'

'Aye,' Middleton said. 'She last e-mailed, let's see...' Middleton clicked on the *Mail* icon on his MacBook. 'Here we are... Friday, 6 March. In it she tells me she's arriving in Edinburgh on the eleventh. I gave her my phone number by return, told her to ring me.'

'The phone she called you on,' Knox said. 'It was a mobile?'

'My iPhone, yes.'

'Would you mind checking its call register, let me have the number?'

'Sure,' Middleton said. He took a mobile phone from a jacket on a nearby coat hook, switched it on, and scanned through its records. A moment or two later he scribbled a number and handed it over. 'There you go,' he said.

'Thank you,' Knox replied.

'Was Laura on her own when you met?' McCann asked.

'Aye, just her.'

'What was she wearing?'

'An orange-coloured parka. No, wait – yellow. The interior lights in The Filling Station have a bit of an orange cast to them.'

'She had a backpack with her?' Knox asked.

Middleton shook his head emphatically. 'Backpack? No, definitely not.'

'How long were you together?'

'A little over an hour.' Middleton paused for a moment and added, 'We began by talking about genealogy, Scottish emigration and the like. Then I asked if she was enjoying her visit, she told me she was.'

'Did she mention anyone she'd met in the course of her visit?' Knox asked.

Middleton paused, his brow furrowing. 'No, no I don't think so.'

'What about where she was staying? Did she talk about that?'

Middleton shrugged. 'Only to say it was a pleasant enough place.'

'What about travel plans?'

'Oh, aye, we discussed those,' Middleton said. 'She said she intended to hire a car the next day. Saturday. Asked if I could recommend a company. I told her Cityhire in

Tollcross are quite well regarded. They've an up-to-date fleet, and are not too expensive.'

'How long did she intend staying in the city?' McCann asked.

'Until Monday, when she intended heading west. Asked if I knew a route to Mull that would let her see something of the Clyde coast. I suggested she drive to Ardrossan, take a ferry to Arran, and cross to Kintyre via Lochranza.'

'And it was definitely Monday, 16 March she intended leaving,' Knox asked. 'Not earlier?'

Middleton shook his head. 'No. She told me she'd paid her B&B five days in advance.'

A commis chef poked his head around the door at that moment and said, 'Chef wants you in the kitchen, Mr Middleton.'

'Aye right, son,' Middleton replied. 'Tell him I'll only be a minute.'

'One more thing, Mr Middleton,' Knox said. 'Where were you on Friday the thirteenth?'

'You don't think—'

'I've got to ask... you understand,' Knox said.

'Aye, I suppose,' Middleton said. 'I was here until well after midnight. Late graduation do for the restaurant owner's daughter. You can check if you like.'

Knox acknowledged this with a nod and the detectives got to their feet. 'Okay,' he said. 'We'll let you get on – thanks for your cooperation.' He took a card from his pocket, handed it over, and added, 'If you recall anything else, please don't hesitate to give us a ring.'

'I will, I promise,' Middleton said. 'And I hope it won't be long until you find Miss Winter's killer.'

* * *

He picked her up just before six and drove via High Street to Castlehill, parked on the right of the Esplanade and exited the car. He then went to the perimeter wall where he began to point out landmarks.

'On this side we're looking north,' he told her. 'Princes Street and Princes Street Gardens are immediately below us. Beyond that the New Town, and beyond that the Firth of Forth and Fife. On a *very* clear day you can see Highland peaks: Ben Lomond and Schiehallion in Perth and Kinross.'

'It's a magnificent view,' Mullen said. 'You know, I've heard people talk about the New Town. I've always wondered why it was called that, when it's clearly Victorian.'

'Georgian and Victorian,' he said with a laugh. 'Built between the mid-eighteenth and mid-nineteenth century.' He waved towards the entrance to the Esplanade. 'We're on the top of a ridge that extends from the castle to the bottom of the Royal Mile, where Holyrood Palace is situated. The Old Town consists of scores of tenements built on either side. By the late seventeenth century it was becoming so populous that the only solution was to build upwards – resulting in tenements five, six and seven stories high.'

'Everyone living cheek by jowl?' she said.

'Yes,' he said. 'Rich merchants and street sweepers; all sharing the same building.'

'Wow,' Mullen said.

'Yeah, and as you can imagine, not very acceptable to those who could afford better.' He nodded in the direction of Princes Street. 'The solution was to build on fields just across from the castle. A new town conceived by lord provost George Drummond, and begun by architect James Craig in 1763.'

Mullen laughed. 'You're well versed on Edinburgh's history,' she said.

'Now, yes,' he agreed. 'But it wasn't until I began with 2Ucabs that I started studying it – after being asked so many questions I couldn't answer. Paid off, too: folk often ask me to take them on city tours.'

They got back in the car and drove down the Royal Mile, passing the Scottish Parliament and entering Holyrood Park on the same stretch of road he'd driven on that morning. This time he turned right into a section of Queen's Drive which encircled Arthur's Seat, a 823-foot peak at the centre of the city. He carried on past a stretch of water called Dunsapie Loch, and came to a stop overlooking Salisbury Crags, a sill of cliffs facing Edinburgh Castle.

'My, but the view from here is incredible,' she said, pointing ahead. 'That's the castle immediately in front of us?'

'Yes,' he replied. 'And the Old Town. The sunset framing its silhouette.'

Mullen said nothing for a few moments, then turned to face him. 'Thank you for showing me the city, Raymond. It's been marvellous.'

He smiled at her and replied, 'I'm glad you enjoyed it, Cassie.' Then, checking his watch, he added, 'You hungry?'

'A little,' she said. 'The Brunstane's dining room is open till nine. I'll get something when I return.'

He nodded to the park's exit road. 'Reason I ask is there's a nice little restaurant a five-minute drive from here. I'd be honoured if you'd have dinner with me.'

'That's kind of you, Raymond, but really I—'

'Please,' he interrupted.

She broke into a smile and said, 'On one condition.'

'Okay.'

'No haggis,' she said. 'I had some last time I was here and it turned my stomach. I know others like it, but I appear to be allergic.'

He grinned and said, 'No haggis.'

* * *

In the event they had Scotch T-bone steak with oven-dried tomatoes and cos lettuce garnished with garlic and thyme, followed by cranachan, a dessert made with oats, raspberries, fresh cream and a dash of Laphroaig whisky.

Mullen finished the sweet, pushed the dish away, and patted her midriff. 'Thank you, Raymond,' she said. 'The meal was delicious.'

He smiled. 'Better than haggis?'

She laughed. 'Much, much better.'

She glanced in the direction of the ladies' room then and added, 'Now if you'll excuse me, I need to powder my nose.'

He watched her go and settled back into his chair, feeling more relaxed than he had in days. The worries weighing on him a mere twenty-four hours ago appeared to have lifted from his shoulders. The nightmare, too, had faded; the concerns that had prompted his visit to St Bridget's also gone from his mind.

He thought about the Canadian girl's actions on the night he'd been possessed: her French-kissing had attracted the evil, he was sure of that now.

He wasn't a prude, but she'd taken him by surprise. They'd only begun kissing when he felt her hand on his crotch. She unzipped his fly, felt his tumescence and removed her jeans and knickers.

He'd been taken aback at her readiness to have intercourse. A bit of foreplay had been necessary with most women he'd had sex with to bring them to the point where they were ready.

If they were ready, that is.

For he never pushed it, ever: if a woman said no, he always pulled back. At no point in his life had he been guilty of rape, and that included Amanda Madden, the girl who had seduced him shortly after his sixteenth birthday.

'Wasn't too long, was I?' Mullen said, returning to her seat and jolting him out of his reverie.

'No,' he said. 'Not at all.'

At that moment their waiter approached with a wine list. 'Would you care to order anything?' he asked. 'Sir, Madam?'

'Cassie?' he said. 'They do a very nice pinot noir.'

'No,' she replied. 'Better not. I'm seeing buyers first thing, I'd like to keep a clear head. May I have coffee instead?'

'You're sure?' he said. A couple of glasses wouldn't do any harm.'

'No, honestly,' she insisted. 'I'm not much of a drinker.'

He smiled and turned to the waiter. 'Just coffee, please.'

The man gave a little bow. 'Fine, sir. Pot of coffee for two.'

After the waiter returned and poured their coffees, she smiled at him and said, 'Well, what do you think?'

'Sorry, Cassie, I'm not with you.'

'It isn't wafting in your direction?'

'What isn't?'

She reached into her handbag, took out a small bottle, and placed it on the table. 'My company's new scent,' she said. 'Produced in partnership with one of the most esteemed perfume producers in Grasse, near Cannes. I sprayed a little on my neck when I was in the ladies' room.'

He sniffed the air, 'Yes, I can smell it now,' he said. 'Nice.'

'Not too overpowering?'

'No,' he said. 'Very pleasant.'

She picked up the bottle. 'No name yet – as you can see the bottle's unlabelled. I'll be showing it to buyers tomorrow, hoping for advance orders. My firm's unsure what to call it. Our MD suggested a name, but unfortunately it's already in use.'

'Really?' he said. 'Which one?'

'Calvin Klein,' she replied. 'Possession.'

He gasped as she said the word, feeling an icy cold run up his spine.

'Raymond,' she said in surprise. 'You've gone as white as a sheet. Are you feeling all right?'

It took a moment to regain his composure. 'Yes,' he said, nodding to the coffee cup. 'Caffeine. It sometimes brings on my migraine.'

'I'm sorry,' she said. 'It's my fault, I should've gone with the wine.'

He shook his head. 'No, Cassie, it isn't. I simply forgot how it affects me.' He paused, adding, 'It'll pass. It always does.'

'You're sure?'

'Yes,' he said.

She glanced at her watch. 'Thanks for a marvellous tour, Raymond,' she said. 'And a lovely meal. But it's twenty past ten and I'd like to make an early start tomorrow. You don't mind?'

'Of course not,' he said. 'I'll run you back to your hotel. But, on the way there, I'd like to show you a view you really don't want to miss: a panorama taking in Arthur's Seat, Salisbury Crags, the Old Town and the castle.' He paused. 'The car park next to the observatory at Blackford Hill. A ten-minute drive.'

'But it's dark,' she said.

'That's just it: the city lights illuminate the sky from Leith to the southern suburbs – you'll see everything.'

She hesitated, again glancing at her watch. 'It's not out of the way?'

'No, it isn't, I promise.'

'Okay,' she said.

They left the restaurant, and ten minutes later were approaching Blackford Hill via a steep incline called Observatory Road. There was only one other car when they arrived in the parking area, which drove off as soon as they came to a stop.

He switched off the engine and pointed to the necklace of lights brightening the night sky. 'There,' he said. 'Well worth the diversion, don't you think?'

'You're right,' she said. 'It's an amazing skyline.'

'I knew you'd like it.' He leaned closer, kissed her and placed a hand on her breast, which she pushed away. 'No, Raymond,' she said. He kissed her a second time and again she pulled back. 'No,' she repeated.

'I thought you liked me,' he said.

'I do, Raymond, but–'

'You're seeing someone else?' he said, sounding irritated.

She nodded. 'Yes, I was engaged. We broke it off a month ago.' A pause. 'I'm not ready for another relationship yet.'

'Oh,' he said disconsolately.

'Look, Raymond, I had a wonderful evening, I really did. I'm sorry if you thought there was something more to it. Will you take me back now?'

'Of course,' he said.

'Thank you.' She leant over and pecked him on the cheek. The scarf she was wearing parted, revealing her neck, and he smelt her perfume.

Possession.

All of a sudden he saw a blinding flash, and Mullen's face was replaced by that of Amanda Madden, who gave him a long, seductive and smouldering look.

Her voice began to echo in his head: "Want to meet up, Raymond? Want to – want to?"

'You bitch,' he said, placing his hands around Mullen's throat. 'You led me on.'

'Stop it,' she exclaimed. 'You're hurting me.'

But it was Amanda's voice he heard, mocking him. "Come on, Raymond," she taunted, "you know you want to."

He became enraged. 'You bitch,' he said. His thumbs were now firmly around Mullen's throat, and he began squeezing harder.

'No!' she said, her voice little more than a croak. 'No-o!'

'You bitch,' he repeated. 'You dirty, fucking little bitch.'

Chapter Ten

'Inspector Cox from the Public Liaison office is with Mrs Winter in an anteroom at the top of the corridor,' Lucy Carmichael was saying. It was a little after 5pm, and she'd just admitted Knox into the Cowgate Mortuary.

'She's seen her daughter's body?' he asked.

'Yes, they've just left the viewing room.'

'How's she taking it?' Knox said.

'She was quiet,' Carmichael replied. 'Composed. It's like that with some folk. Able to keep their grief bottled up – for a while, at least.'

Knox thumbed towards the other end of the corridor. 'I'd better go and speak to her.'

'I'll be in the office when you're done,' Carmichael said. 'I was about to put the kettle on – you'll have a cup of tea?'

Knox nodded enthusiastically. 'Aye, please,' he said. 'I'll be in need of one.'

A moment later, Knox reached the room where the women were waiting. Two uniformed officers sat on a leather sofa flanking a third person, a woman in her sixties, whose black-bagged eyes bore testimony to her distress.

On a coffee table in front lay a silver teapot, cups, and a plate of biscuits which appeared untouched.

Inspector Cox looked up as he entered and said, 'Jack.'

'Beth,' Knox replied. Then to her sergeant, he added, 'Lydia.'

The sergeant dipped her head in acknowledgement, and Cox turned to the woman alongside her. 'Catherine,' she said, 'this is Detective Inspector Knox, the officer in charge of the investigation.'

Knox pulled a seat from the wall and sat down as the woman glanced in his direction. 'Mrs Winter,' he said. 'Pleased to meet you.'

'Can't say I feel the same, given the circumstances,' she replied. 'No offence.'

'I understand,' Knox said. 'None taken.'

The sergeant indicated the woman's cup. 'Would you like a top-up, Catherine?'

Mrs Winter shook her head and addressed Knox, 'Do you know who Laura's killer is?'

'Not yet, no,' Knox replied.

'Can't be too difficult,' she said bitterly. 'She'd only been in the country four days.'

'I agree,' Knox said. 'We're doing everything possible to discover who your daughter came in contact with, and I'm sure our inquiries will lead us to something soon.' He paused. 'Forensics are helping in that direction, Mrs Winter, but there's a couple of things you might be able to add. We didn't find Laura's mobile – could you let us have the number?'

Mrs Winter made to reach for her handbag, but Cox took a pen from the sleeve of her tunic as her sergeant placed a notebook on the table. 'Here, Catherine,' she said. 'Use this.'

Winter began writing and glanced up at Knox. 'You want her e-mail address, too?'

'Please,' Knox replied.

She scribbled for a moment, tore off the sheet, and handed it to Knox.

'Thank you,' he said, and compared it with the slip Middleton had given him and saw that the numbers matched.

'You said a *couple* of things?' Mrs Winter asked.

'Yes,' Knox said. 'When did you last speak to Laura?'

'On Friday, 13 March. It was just after eight in the morning at home so it must have been after 1pm here.'

'Do you remember what you talked about?' Knox asked.

'Clearly,' Mrs Winter replied. 'She told me she was meeting the man from the Caledonian Heritage Group…' She paused. 'I can't remember his name.'

'Middleton,' Knox said.

'Ah, yes, Middleton. She told me she had arranged to meet and thank him for helping trace my grandfather's place of birth. I'd also been curious, as my father left my mother soon after I was born.'

'How long did you talk for?'

'Around ten minutes.'

'Laura didn't mention anyone else?'

'No, only Middleton.'

Knox gave a nod of acknowledgement and she added, 'I'd like to make arrangements to have Laura taken home, how long will you need to keep her here?'

'We should be able to let you go ahead soon,' Knox replied. 'You're staying at a hotel?'

'Yes. The Calton on North Bridge.'

'I've taken Mrs Winter's contact details,' Cox said.

'Right,' Knox replied.

'You'll let me know when you discover who did it?' Mrs Winter said.

'I'll be in touch the moment we make an arrest,' Knox assured her.

Cox got to her feet and gently tapped Mrs Winter's hand. 'Come on, Catherine,' she said. 'Lydia and I will drive you to your hotel.'

* * *

Back at the office a steaming-hot mug of tea was waiting. 'I poured in some milk,' Carmichael said. 'Wasn't sure if you took sugar.'

Knox joined her at the table and stirred in a couple of heaped teaspoons. 'Two,' he said.

Carmichael gave him an indulgent look. 'More like three.'

'Aye, well…' Knox left it hanging.

She nodded towards the corridor. 'Rough?'

Knox shook his head. 'Doesn't get easier.'

'Mrs Winter held up okay?'

'Just.'

He gulped down some tea, replaced the mug on the table and pointed to an empty desk at the opposite end of the room. 'Alex finished early?'

'Took the afternoon off,' Carmichael replied. 'Able to, now he has me.'

Knox nodded. 'How are you finding it?'

She shrugged. 'Pretty much the same in terms of work, only the environment has changed.'

'You prefer Dundee?'

'No, it's not that. Takes time to settle in.'

'Promotion, though?' Knox said. 'You'll be taking charge?'

'Oh, yes, happy I made the move. It's just… well, friends and such, making the adjustment.'

'You were in a relationship?' Knox said, then quickly caught himself. 'Sorry – you don't need to answer. I'm being personal.'

'I don't mind,' Carmichael said. 'I divorced five years ago, after I found out my husband was having an affair.

Not entirely his fault. I was working long hours, seldom home.'

'Sounds familiar,' Knox said.

'You, too?'

'Uh-huh; the long hours, not an affair. Divorced in 2007. Susan's in Australia, as is my son, Jamie. We're still on good terms.'

'Yes, it ended quite amicably for me, too.'

'Any children?'

Carmichael shook her head. 'No,' she replied, took a sip of tea, and added, 'How old is your son?'

'Twenty-nine.'

She tilted her head slightly, looked directly at him, and smiled. 'You don't look old enough.'

Knox gave a sardonic grin. 'I am, though. Have a granddaughter, too.'

'Really?' she said. 'What's her name?'

'Lily,' he said. 'Three last January. She's a cutie.'

'I'm sure you all dote on her,' Carmichael said.

'We do.' Knox drained his mug and set it back on the table. 'You were telling me yesterday you were moving into a flat at Ratcliffe Terrace?'

'Yes,' she said. 'The deal went through today and I move in next week. I'll be glad, I'm currently renting a room in a multiple occupancy flat in Jeffrey Street. Central, but a bit cramped.'

'Yeah, far from ideal,' Knox said. He gazed at her for a long moment, and added, 'Look, Lucy, I was wondering if—'

The ringtone of his mobile went off at that moment and he took the device from his pocket. He checked the screen and said, 'My boss. Excuse me while I take it.'

'Of course,' Carmichael said.

Knox pressed *accept*. 'Sir?' he said.

'Jack,' Warburton replied. 'Where are you?'

'Cowgate Mortuary,' Knox replied. 'Spoke to Mrs Winter. She was able to give me Laura's mobile number.'

Warburton's tone warned him there was something amiss. 'Problem, sir?'

'Afraid so. Just had a call from HQ. A resident in Strathearn Grove found a body near the Royal Observatory. Officers from Howdenhall are in attendance and the locus has been secured. I rang DS McCann, asked her to meet you there.'

'Uniform were able to ID the body?'

'Only to say it was a young woman in her mid to late twenties.'

As Warburton spoke, the telephone on Carmichael's desk rang. As she picked up and began talking, Warburton continued, 'HQ tells me they've been in touch with DI Murray and DS Beattie. They're contacting the pathologist, too.'

Knox glanced at Carmichael, who was taking notes.

'Yes, sir, I think they're speaking to her now.'

'*Her?*' Warburton said.

'Yes, sir,' Knox replied. 'Alex Turley's off duty. I'm with Lucy Carmichael, the lady who's taking over from him.'

'Ah, right,' Warburton said. 'Okay, I'll leave it with you.' There was a short silence, and he added, 'Two young women in two days, Jack. Bad omen. Hope we don't have a serial murderer on our hands.'

* * *

A young constable waved Knox through the barrier tape and he took a space in the observatory parking lot, which was empty save for two police cars and DI Murray's Range Rover.

As Knox exited, the forensic officer greeted him. 'The girl was found on a bank of grass below,' he told Knox. 'Tent's erected. Just waiting for the pathologist.'

Knox thumbed towards a dark-blue Honda Accord, which was just entering the car park. 'She's here,' he said. 'I was at Cowgate Mortuary when Warburton phoned. She followed me here.'

'Alex Turley's not on duty?'

'Afternoon off,' Knox replied. 'Ms Carmichael's his replacement.'

'Yes, I heard he was retiring,' Murray said.

Carmichael exited her car and walked over. 'Someone mention my name?' she said.

'Lucy, this is DI Ed Murray, SPA Forensics,' Knox said.

At that moment DS Beattie emerged from the opposite side of the Range Rover and joined them. 'And this DS Liz Beattie, his more-than-able assistant.'

Knox nodded to the pathologist. 'This is Lucy Carmichael, Liz, the lady who's taking over from Alex later this year.'

They shook hands and Beattie said, 'Watch out for this man, Lucy, he's a flatterer.'

'Really?' Carmichael said, grinning. 'Well, you know what they say; it'll get you anywhere.' She pursed her lips and pointed to the verge. 'The locus?'

'Aye,' Murray said. 'Ledge of grass a short distance down the hill. Uniform have tented the body and pegged off the immediate area.'

'You began any tests?'

'No,' Murray said. 'Thought it better to wait until you'd done a preliminary examination.'

'Okay,' Carmichael said, gesturing towards the Honda. 'I'll get my coveralls and take a look.'

As she walked off, Knox said, 'DS McCann's arrived yet?'

'Arrived before us,' Beattie replied. 'She's at the other side of the observatory, interviewing Mr Randall.'

'Mr Randall?'

'The man who found the body.'

'Oh,' Knox said. 'I didn't see her car as I drove in.'

'I think she parked around the side,' Beattie said.

Murray nodded over Knox's shoulder. 'Here she is now.'

Knox turned and saw McCann approach. 'Arlene,' he said. 'Warburton made you miss Eastenders?'

McCann smiled. 'You're so old-fashioned, boss,' she said. 'There are wee electronic boxes nowadays, allow you to watch at anytime.'

Knox shrugged. 'Aye, I suppose I am a bit of a Luddite.' He nodded towards the corner of the observatory. 'You spoke to the man who found her?'

'Aye,' McCann said. 'A Mr Miles Randall, 19 Strathearn Grove. An amateur photographer, he arrived at the observatory just after 6pm to photograph the sunset. He told me he was using a tripod-mounted Intrepid 8x10 camera. Whatever that is.'

'Large format,' Murray said. 'Single sheet of film negative per exposure; hence 8x10. Hefty piece of kit.'

'You let him go, Arlene?' Knox asked.

'Yes,' McCann replied. 'Said we might need to talk to him later.'

Knox nodded. 'The girl, we know who she is yet?'

'PC Newman, one of the first officers on the scene, found her handbag,' Murray replied. 'Put on a pair of nitrile gloves and brought it to me. I was checking the contents when you arrived.'

'And?'

'A driving licence and several business cards were among the contents. Identifies her as Cassandra Mullen, aged twenty-five. The cards reveal she was a sales rep for a cosmetics company in Kensington, called Leonis. The licence gives her place of residence as 29 Gardner Street, Poole, Dorset.'

'Did Newman say where he found the bag?'

'Clump of bushes near the body. No real attempt to hide it, apparently. Newman thinks whoever killed her threw it there.'

'Mobile phone?' Knox said.

'Yeah, there's one in her handbag,' Beattie said. 'We haven't got around to checking it.'

Knox walked to the verge, studied the ground, and turned to McCann.

'Randall told you where he positioned his tripod?' he asked.

'Yes,' McCann said. 'He told me he took several pictures at the verge where you're standing, then moved his car to the opposite side of the observatory, where I spoke to him. He was setting up there when he realised he was missing a filter...' McCann paused and checked her notebook. 'A polariser, he said it was.'

Murray nodded. 'Yes, suppresses glare,' he said. 'Slots into a holder in front of the lens.'

Knox cast his eyes over the darkening skyline. 'Quite a view.' He paused for a moment and added, 'Randall told you he parked here first, Arlene?'

'Yes. But didn't notice the girl's body until he walked back to retrieve the filter.'

'M-hmm,' Knox said. 'Five designated spaces, fifty or so yards from the main car park. Obvious spot if you had a heavy camera in the boot and intended photographing the scene.'

'Or wanted to take in the view but didn't intend leaving the car,' McCann said.

Knox nodded. 'Exactly.' He pointed to where the tent was positioned. 'I'm going to speak to the pathologist. Should be able to tell us how Ms Mullen died.'

'You think she was strangled, boss?' McCann said.

'I do,' Knox said. 'Which will confirm the DCI's fears — that Laura Winter and Cassandra Mullen were murdered by the same person.'

Chapter Eleven

A large spotlight powered by a portable generator illuminated the tent's interior, clearly outlining Carmichael's shadow. A constable standing outside tipped a finger to his hat as Knox approached. 'Sir,' he said.

Knox acknowledged the man with a nod and cleared his throat. 'Okay to come inside, Lucy?' he said.

'Yes,' she replied. 'Almost done.'

Knox pulled back the flysheet, entered, and saw the pathologist kneeling over the corpse of a young woman, which lay prone. The victim was wearing a floral skirt that had been hitched to her waist.

Carmichael was easing a pair of briefs over the deceased's hips. 'I've just taken a vaginal swab,' she said, placing a small plastic container into a bag at her side. 'Negative for semen.'

'Sexual assault wasn't attempted?' Knox said.

Carmichael swung around and pointed to a dark-blue coat and a yellow scarf, which had been placed next to the body.

'The forensics officers will want to examine her clothing for semen traces,' she said. 'But, no, doesn't look like it.'

'Cause of death?'

Carmichael pointed to a dark red weal encircling the woman's throat. 'Strangulation. Considerable degree of pressure on the trachea. Second time I've seen that type of injury this week.'

'Laura Winter was the first?'

'Yes.'

'How long has she lain here?'

'I'll need to take a more detailed look, but going by lividity in the back of her neck, trunk and limbs, I'd guess twenty hours.'

Knox did a mental calculation. 'Around ten last night?' he said.

'Give or take.'

'No other injury?'

'You mean had she been beaten in any way?'

'Yes.'

'Not that I can see,' Carmichael replied. 'Only other marks are on the backs of her heels. Slight scratches where her tights are torn; result of her being dragged.'

'Tarmac at the car park,' Knox said.

'Probably,' Carmichael replied. She paused. 'The officers found her handbag?'

'Yes, Liz told me they have it.'

Carmichael stood. 'Okay,' she said. 'I'll hand the scene over to Ed and Liz and arrange to have her picked up as soon as they've completed the photography and videography. Give me a ring tomorrow, Jack. I'll commence the PM tonight, update you by lunchtime.'

* * *

As Carmichael drove out of the car park Murray turned to Knox and said, 'Liz and I had a more detailed look at the five spaces near the verge, Jack. If the killer parked there – which is likely – we thought his tyres might've left an impression. But it's mostly fine, loose gravel. Yielded nothing of interest.'

79

Knox motioned towards the tent. 'Might find something on her clothes,' he said. Then to Beattie, he added, 'You checked her phone, Liz?'

'Yes,' Beattie replied. 'I gave it to Arlene to follow up.'

'Aye, boss,' McCann said, and held up the device with a gloved hand. Among those listed are her Mum and Dad. Other contacts include Stephen, Audrey, Lindsay and Office. I've been in touch with Linked, the service provider. Their customer services tell me her parents' number is a landline in Poole. The others are in London, including the last, in Kensington. Also a landline; her office, presumably.'

'Recent numbers dialled?'

'Only three, all outgoing: one to Audrey, presumably a friend, the other to her parents, both made between 9.48am and 10.17am yesterday.'

'They gave locations?'

'Yeah,' McCann said. 'One in the Darlington area, the other 12 miles north of Morpeth.'

Knox gave her a puzzled look.

'It'll make sense in a minute, boss,' McCann said. 'When I tell you about the final call.'

'Go on,' Knox said.

'2Ucabs, the taxi hire company. She called them at 11.02am from the Waverley station.'

Knox dipped his head in understanding. 'She was on a train.'

'Yeah,' McCann said. 'I checked. East Coast line: their six o'clock from London King's Cross; got in at 10.47am.'

'And that was the only call she made? No other calls after she arrived at her hotel?'

McCann shook her head. 'Nothing. I gave Brunstane Hotel a ring and spoke to the receptionist who booked her in. She told me Ms Mullen took lunch and went to her room. Didn't see her again until early evening, when she asked about the last sitting for dinner. She went out soon afterwards.'

'The receptionist see who picked her up?'

'Said she was busy at the time, didn't notice.'

'And the call to 2Ucabs at eleven was definitely the last she made?'

'Yes,' McCann said.

Knox turned to Murray. 'Okay, Ed,' he said. 'We'll give you the mobile and let you and Liz get on.'

Beattie took the phone from McCann, placed it in an evidence bag, and Murray said, 'We'll do a thorough check on that and her other gear.' He thumbed towards the tent. 'I'll get Howdenhall to send down some extra bodies, too, soon as it's light. Do a fingertip search. You never know, he might've discarded something.'

Knox nodded in acknowledgment. 'Thanks, Ed. You'll let me know if you find anything of interest?'

'As soon as, Jack, absolutely.'

* * *

Knox and his team gathered in the office after nine the following morning. He reconfigured the whiteboard into two sections: Laura Winter's data on the left, a vertical line, and Cassandra Mullen's on the right.

'Okay,' he said. 'We're agreed, same killer. Same MO with regard to the way the girls met their deaths.' He turned to the others and added, 'Any thoughts?'

'Laura Winters was semi-naked,' McCann said, 'Although sexual intercourse hadn't taken place, she appears to have been willing.'

'Right,' Knox said. 'Go on.'

'Completely different scenario with Cassandra Mullen. Her body is fully clothed. Why?'

'She rejected his advances?' Fulton said.

'Possible,' McCann replied. 'But why accompany him to a secluded spot such as Blackford Hill?'

'To indulge in a bit of necking,' Hathaway volunteered. 'Decided she didn't want to go further?'

'No, not that. I think there's another reason,' McCann said. 'Location.'

'Of course,' Knox agreed. 'He parked in the same spot where Randall took his pictures the following evening – he was showing her the view.'

Fulton made a face. 'Really, boss?' he said. 'At ten o'clock at night?'

'You're the city expert, Bill,' Knox said. 'You're bound to have seen the outlook from there.'

'Aye,' Fulton said. 'Bonnie vista during the day, I'll grant you. But after dark?'

Knox grinned. 'Then you're missing out, Bill. Even at night it's quite a sight, I assure you.' He paused. 'Okay. Two girls, both strangers to the city. Only here a few days – how do they meet their killer?'

'Someone at the Waverley Station?' Hathaway said. 'Laura spent some time at the tourist board there, and Cassandra arrived by train.'

'Unlikely,' Knox said. 'In any event, Cassandra Mullen arrived at 10.47. She called the taxi company eighteen minutes later.'

'No connection with where they were staying?' Fulton said.

'Don't think so,' Knox replied. 'Other than the owners, Laura spoke only to Peabody, at the Sea View. And Middleton, the genealogy guy.' Knox tapped the whiteboard, and continued, 'After arriving at the Brunstane, Cassandra spent the afternoon in her room. The only other person who came into contact with both women were the taxi drivers who took them to their destinations.'

'Of course,' McCann said. '2Ucabs. Same driver?'

'Possible,' Knox said and turned to Hathaway. 'Give them a ring and check it, will you, Mark?'

'Boss.'

'Okay,' Knox said. 'Anything else?'

'One thing is bothering me,' McCann said. 'Laura's backpack. She takes it with her when she goes, yet leaves a dresser strewn with cosmetics. Very odd.'

'You think she didn't take it?'

'Yes,' McCann said. 'I've a feeling Willie Carter's hiding something.'

'I'm inclined to agree,' Knox said. He took a slip of paper from his pocket and gave it to Fulton. 'Locate the service provider of this number, will you, Bill?' he said. 'It's Laura Winter's, so most likely a Canadian company. Would be useful if we were able to pinpoint where it was last used.'

'I'll get right onto it,' Fulton said.

Hathaway replaced the handset of his phone and addressed Knox. 'You're right, boss,' he said. '2Ucabs say Laura Winter and Cassandra Mullen were picked up by the same driver.'

'Who?' Knox asked.

'Someone called George Banks.'

'Address?'

'182 Logie Green Road,' Hathaway replied.

Knox checked his watch. 'Mm-hmm,' he said and turned to Fulton. 'Logie Green Road, Bill, that's near Powderhall, isn't it?'

'Aye,' Fulton confirmed. 'Off Broughton Road, a ten-minute drive.'

'Right,' Knox said. 'Arlene and I will pay him a visit.' He glanced at Hathaway. 'Mark, get on to DI Murray. Ask him to give me a ring, will you? Might need more detail on the tyre prints at Pathhead.'

* * *

Knox and McCann were leaving the station when two men entered the reception area. The taller of the two glanced at Knox and said, 'DI Jack Knox, isn't it?'

Knox turned to face the man. 'Yes,' he replied.

'Thought I recognised you,' he said. 'I'm Reggie Collins, I was a DI at St Leonards when you came up from Peebles in the 1990s. Moved on a month later to the Fettes office.'

Knox studied the speaker for a moment. Last time they'd met he'd been slimmer and had worn a thin moustache. 'Yes, I remember, sir,' he said. 'You look different.'

Collins smiled and patted his midriff. 'Aye,' he said. 'A few pounds heavier and less facial hair, eh?' He pointed to the stairway behind Knox. 'Is DCI Warburton at home?'

'Yes, sir,' Knox replied. 'In his office.'

'Good,' he replied. He and his companion crossed the hallway and Collins added, 'Nice to see you again, Jack.'

A minute later Knox got into his car and McCann followed, clicking her seatbelt into place. 'Complaints?' she said.

'Aye,' Knox replied. 'When Bill told me who interviewed him, his name didn't ring a bell.' Knox started the car, moved off, and added, 'Like he said, left St Leonards soon after I arrived.'

'Who's his dour-faced sidekick?'

'DI Dave Simmonds,' Knox replied. 'I don't know him, but Collins is okay. Word on the grapevine is that he's fair.'

'He'll be giving the chief the outcome of their investigation into Bill's case?'

Knox nodded. 'Likely.'

'Then I only hope it's good news,' McCann said. 'I didn't like the look on that Simmonds bugger's face.'

Chapter Twelve

The address at Logie Green Road was situated in a corner block at the junction of Warriston Road, near a river known as the Water of Leith. Knox and McCann went to the entrance, where Knox studied names listed beside an intercom. He pressed a buzzer marked "G. Banks", received no answer, then pressed a second time, keeping his thumb on the button.

'Aye, aye, aye,' a voice responded moments later. 'Where's the bloody fire?'

'Mr George Banks?' Knox asked.

'Aye, who's asking?'

'Detective Inspector Knox. I wonder if you could talk to us for a minute?'

'*Us?*'

'Yes,' Knox replied. 'Myself and my colleague, Detective Sergeant McCann.'

'What about?'

'I'd be in a better position to answer if we could speak face-to-face.'

'Eh? Oh, right, wait a minute.' The buzzer sounded, and Banks added, 'Third floor, second door.'

The detectives ascended the stairs and arrived at the third floor. Banks stood at the far door, wearing pale blue pyjamas and a checked dressing gown. He was a small man; stocky and almost completely bald. Knox guessed him to be in his early thirties.

Banks opened the door wider and nodded towards the end of a short hallway. 'Come in,' he said. 'The living room's at the top.'

Banks closed the door and ushered them into the living room, waving to a settee. 'You'd better take a seat,' he said.

The detectives did so and Banks took a chair next to a dining table. 'Can't be to do with the bump I had in the Grassmarket,' he said. 'Gave all my details to the cop at the scene. Me and the van driver exchanged addresses. I was told the insurance would sort it out.'

Knox shook his head. 'That's not why we're here.'

Banks made a face. 'No?'

'You work for 2Ucabs?' Knox asked.

Banks's brow furrowed and he leaned forward slightly. 'Of course.'

'We spoke to your office this morning,' Knox said. 'They tell us you picked up a Ms Laura Winter at 4.39pm on March 11. Drove her to the Sea View Guest House in Links Place. And on Monday this week, 23 March, you met a Ms Cassandra Mullen at the Waverley Station at 11.14am. Took her to the Brunstane Hotel on Milton Road East.'

Banks shook his head. '2Ucabs is a busy outfit,' he said. 'Most days I'm on the go the entire shift. Can't recall every fare, to be honest.'

'You don't remember picking up a young woman at the Waverley only two days ago?' McCann asked.

Banks shrugged. 'If you're anywhere near the centre of town that's where you'll be called to. Punters come and go to the station all day.' He shook his head. 'Sorry, can't say I do.' Banks gave Knox a quizzical look and added, 'These women,' he said. 'Something's happened to them?'

'Afraid so,' Knox replied. 'Both were murdered.'

'Christ!' Banks said, his eyes widening. 'And you believe I had something to do with it?'

'I don't believe anything at the moment,' Knox said. 'Only that 2Ucabs tell us you were the driver who drove the women to their destinations.' Knox took out his notebook, leafed through it, and found the page he was looking for. 'I'd like you to cast your mind back,' he said. 'Laura Winter was Canadian, had a backpack with her. Cassandra Mullen booked into the Brunstane around 11.30am.'

Banks glanced towards the ceiling and was quiet for a moment. 'No, I'm sorry,' he said. 'To tell the truth, March has been really busy. No sooner have I set down a fare and the app beeps and it's on to the next.'

'The app?' McCann said.

'Aye,' Banks replied. 'Punters download a 2Ucabs app and click on it when they want a cab. We drivers have one on our smartphones, too. That and a magnetised tracking device that attaches to the dashboard, next to the iPhone. Gives our location to the company computer, which detects if we're free or about to disengage. Alerts us to someone waiting near to where we drop off. Drivers tap on the 2Ucabs icon if they want to accept the fare.' He paused and nodded slowly. 'Now I come to think of it, I recall being at the Brunstane Monday lunchtime. Don't remember anything about the fare, though.'

'Not that she was female?' McCann said.

Banks shrugged. 'I haven't a particularly good memory, to be honest. Like I say, this month's been particularly busy. Some days are just a blur: pick up, drop off; all day long.'

Knox's mobile rang and he glanced at the screen. He saw it was DI Murray, and remembered he'd asked Hathaway to have the forensics officer ring him.

'Excuse me while I take this,' he said to Banks.

'Aye, no worries,' Banks replied. 'Go ahead.'

'Detective Inspector Knox,' he said. The formal reply signalled to Murray that he was in the middle of an interview.

'DC Hathaway told me to give you a ring,' Murray said. 'You're in the presence of someone of interest?'

'Yes,' Knox said.

'Mark mentioned tyre prints. You wanted to know if we can assess a match?'

'Exactly,' Knox said.

'No doubt,' Murray confirmed. 'Clear prints of all four tyres, probably less than two months old. Road chips and the like result in a tread having unique wear patterns – as distinctive as a fingerprint. Scuffing to the nearside front, too, which suggests it's been kerbed at some point.' Murray paused. 'You think it could be linked to the guy you're talking to?'

'Possible,' Knox said.

'Okay. We've a test bed at Howdenhall. Tell him not to move his car; leave it in situ. I'll have a couple of men come over with a low loader, pick it up. I should be able to give you a definitive answer afterwards.'

'Right,' Knox said. 'I'll do that. Thanks.'

He rang off and turned to Banks. 'The car you use with 2Ucabs, it's your only vehicle?'

Banks nodded. 'Aye, a Toyota Prius. Why?'

'We found tyre prints where Ms Winter's body was found. You don't mind if we bring it in for a check?'

'What?' Banks exclaimed. 'You think I'm guilty? I told you, the women's deaths have bugger all to do with me.'

'Then you won't mind us taking a look, will you, sir?' Knox said. 'It'll help us eliminate you.'

* * *

'Sorry, I've a bit of bad news, Sergeant,' Collins was saying. The Professional Standards officer was back in the interview room where Fulton had been questioned two days earlier. DI Simmonds was seated next to the DCI, and Fulton was facing them. 'We spoke to the other two Pick-Pak employees who witnessed Gilliland's arrest,' he continued, 'Gary Neillands, a salesman, and David Toomey, shelf-stacker.'

'What did they see?' Fulton asked.

'Neillands didn't actually witness the arrest,' Collins said. 'He was at the top of the aisle, right enough, but returning a box to a shelf. He had his back to you.'

'Toomey didn't, though,' Simmonds said with a self-satisfied look. 'He corroborates the arrested man's version, contradicting the statement you gave us on Monday. Gilliland fell to the centre of the aisle; contact with the pallet was due to the force of your tackle.'

'That's a damned lie,' Fulton said. 'Where was this Toomey, anyway? I didn't see him.'

'Refilling a gondola stand near the checkouts,' Collins said. 'Heard the commotion, stopped what he was doing, and looked into the aisle.'

'When I made the arrest, I was facing the checkouts,' Fulton said. 'Those immediately opposite were unmanned. I saw no other member of staff.' He paused and added, 'Wilkie was immediately behind me. He *must've* seen what happened.'

'We asked him about his statement again,' Collins said. 'He repeated he couldn't be sure how Gilliland met his injury.'

'Unlike Toomey,' Simmonds said. 'We checked Pik-Pak's CCTV images. He was exactly where he said he was; stacking a gondola at the foot of the aisle.'

'CCTV?' Fulton said, brightening a little. 'Don't the cameras show anything else?'

'Unfortunately, no,' Collins replied. 'The only two working cover the checkouts. We're unlucky; there's a fault in the wiring of those trained on the aisles – they aren't recording. Pik-Pak tells us the maintenance company was scheduled to carry out a repair this week.'

Fulton glanced at Collins for a long moment. 'You began by saying you had bad news?'

Collins placed his hands on the table, palms down. 'You know the case is being pursued by Gilliland's lawyer, Mr Miles Read?'

'Yes,' Fulton replied.

'You're also aware that Read brought it to the attention of Jackie Lyon, and that it featured in her programme *Scotland in Focus* on Monday evening?'

'I am, yes.'

'Well, it's also reached the eyes and ears of the Chief Constable who, to put it mildly, is displeased with the negative attention. He rang this morning and asked for an update. I went over my investigation into Gilliland's arrest; the witnesses' statements, et cetera. Naturally, I had to update him on Toomey's testimony. He asked if I felt it might influence the case against you and I had to admit the possibility. He's asked me to refer the case to the Procurator Fiscal, and to place you on full suspension, effective immediately.'

Fulton shook his head. 'So, that's it: I'm off office duties, too?'

Collins gave a slow but affirmative nod. 'You realise I'll continue to investigate independently of the Procurator Fiscal? The Chief's obviously been influenced by Lyon's programme when arriving at his decision. His prerogative, of course.'

'Makes no difference, does it, sir?' Fulton said. 'I'm still being penalized.'

'Sorry,' Collins said and stood up. Simmonds did likewise, a look of triumph of his face.

'See your boss, Sergeant,' Collins continued. 'DCI Warburton will advise on procedure.'

Fulton waited a few moments after they had departed, then exited the room and found Hathaway waiting. His colleague saw his expression and said, 'Not good news, is it, Sarge?'

Fulton shook his head. 'Full suspension, effective immediately.'

'Damn,' Hathaway said. 'On whose testimony?'

'A shelf-stacker at Pick-Pak. Claims Gilliland received his injury as a result of my arrest.'

'Who is this witness and where was he?'

'A man called Toomey. At the foot of the aisle where I nabbed Gilliland. CCTV proves he was there.'

'But it's his word regarding what he saw?' Hathaway said. 'Doesn't prove he's right.'

'Aye, I agree,' Fulton said. 'An arse-covering exercise. Collins told me the Chief saw Lyon's programme on police brutality. He's signalling the media that Gilliland's allegation is being taken seriously.'

'Still doesn't merit full suspension, Sarge.'

'Won't argue with that,' Fulton said. 'Collins is referring the case to the Procurator Fiscal *and* continuing his investigation. So Toomey will be subject to a more detailed interview – with the union rep's lawyer, too, if it goes to court. I know I'm in the right, Mark; not worried about the outcome.'

Hathaway nodded. 'You've still to see Warburton?'

'Aye, procedure,' Fulton replied. 'Hand over my warrant card and keys to the Astra.'

'Any idea how long you'll be in limbo?'

Fulton shrugged. 'Two weeks, a month. Not to worry, eh? The wife's been nagging about the garden, starting to see some weeds. Time to catch up.' A pause. 'Oh, before I forget, the boss asked me to locate Laura Winter's service provider, find out when her iPhone was last used.'

'You were able to?'

'Aye,' Fulton replied. 'Just before the Complaints guys spoke to me. Left a note on my desk. The company's called Trans-Province Utility. They checked their satellite location software, discovered that her phone was switched on and off again at 11.30am on Saturday, 14 March. At

Links Place – the Sea View Guest House. No calls were made.'

'Half eleven on the fourteenth?' Hathaway said. 'But Laura Winter had already been murdered.'

Fulton winked. 'I know,' he said. 'Interesting, isn't it?'

Chapter Thirteen

He seldom ever drank. The odd pint or two, perhaps, particularly if he was with ex-army mates. On those occasions it was only beer though; never spirits. On Monday night, however, he'd downed almost a third of a bottle of Johnnie Walker to allow him to sleep.

But it had been a fitful slumber, during which he'd awoken several times; heart thumping, panic rising in his throat. And the same nightmarish vision: Cassie slumped in the passenger seat – a wan look on her face. Purple lips flecked with spittle.

The last memory before he blacked out had been the smell of her perfume, and an image of his erstwhile seductress, Amanda, mocking him.

He rose, threw off his pyjamas, went to the bathroom and splashed his face with water. He dressed, made coffee and stared at the wall as he cupped a mug in his hands. Again his worst fears had come to pass, and in almost identical circumstances: he'd taken the life of a young woman, and could remember little about it.

When he came to and saw Mullen's lifeless body he'd sat in silence, fighting panic, gathering his thoughts. After a while he checked to make sure no one was about and dragged her body down the incline. He left it near a clump of bushes, and on his return saw her handbag in the car's footwell. He took a tissue from his pocket, wrapped its handles and threw it into the thicket, then placed the tissue back in his pocket.

He took another gulp of coffee and cast his mind back, pondering on anything that might link him to Mullen.

He'd driven her from the Waverley to the Brunstane Hotel. 2Ucabs would have a record, of course, but there was no need to worry on that score. Not once he'd sorted it out, at least.

He was sure no one had seen him when he dropped her off, nor when he picked her up, which left only the restaurant where they'd had dinner. But he hadn't pre-booked and reasoned it unlikely police would find out.

The contents of her bag? Only her phone. He'd had no need to call her, though, nor she him. Nothing to fear there, either.

He took another swig of coffee and his thoughts returned to his main concern: the malign influence lurking somewhere in his psyche, poised to return if ever he was in a similar situation.

He mustn't allow it the opportunity, that was certain. And that meant no more assignations in places where he was vulnerable to its influence.

He downed the remainder of his coffee, locked up, and took his car out of the garage. His mobile pinged as he switched it on, letting him know of a fare waiting in nearby Stockbridge. A slight jar as the car's wheels reversed over the kerb brought an ache to his temples, reminding him he was still hung-over.

There was little traffic and minutes later he'd arrived at the junction of Hamilton Place and Deanhaugh Street. The lights sequenced to green, and he selected first gear. As the car moved off, he felt a sudden, blinding pain behind his eyes.

Moments later a dark curtain descended, and he lapsed into unconsciousness.

* * *

'Came as a surprise to me, too,' Warburton was telling Knox. He and McCann had returned to Gayfield Square, and the DCI had called him into his office to talk about Fulton's suspension.

'Got to be politics, surely?' Knox said. 'Lyon's programme ruffled the Chief Constable's feathers – censuring Bill takes some of the heat off?'

'The shelf-stacker maintains Gilliland was injured due to the manner of his arrest.'

'But Collins hadn't concluded his investigations, sir,' Knox countered. 'Did he check Toomey's background? Can we be sure the testimony's kosher?'

Warburton shrugged. 'Perhaps not,' he said. 'However, CCTV places him at the end of the aisle, which lends it some credence.'

'Full suspension on the strength of one man's version of events, though,' Knox replied. 'A bit draconian.'

'I know,' Warburton agreed. 'If it were up to me…'

'Sorry, sir,' Knox said. 'I'm not trying to shoot the messenger.'

'I'm aware of that, Jack,' Warburton said. The pair fell silent for a long moment, then Warburton asked, 'DC Hathaway told me you were interviewing someone in connection with the car tracks at Pathhead. How did you get on?'

'I spoke to a George Banks,' Knox replied, 'the 2Ucabs driver who took Laura Winter to Links Place. Same man picked up Cassandra Mullen at the Waverley.'

'What did he tell you?'

'Very little. He doesn't recall either girl.'

'The tyre tracks, good enough for a match?'

Knox nodded. 'Ed assures me they are.'

'He arranged to collect Banks's car?'

'Yes, a couple of lads with a low loader arrived before we left. We should know by this afternoon.'

'This cab driver,' Warburton said. 'What's your feeling?'

'Doesn't appear all that concerned, to be honest,' Knox said.

'Any other leads?'

'Yes. William Carter, proprietor of the Sea View Guest House, is giving cause for suspicion. He insists Laura took her backpack when she left, including mobile phone. Bill ran a check with the Canadian service provider, discovered it was last used on Saturday, 14 March – 11.30am.'

Warburton raised his eyebrows. '*After* her body was found?'

'Yes.'

'Where, they were able to say?'

'Links Place,' Knox replied.

'Really?' Warburton replied. 'You'll see him again?'

'My next port of call,' Knox said, then got to his feet.

Warburton nodded. 'Okay, Jack,' he said. 'Keep me up to speed.'

'Sir,' Knox replied and departed the office.

His attention was immediately drawn to Hathaway, who was seated next to McCann, waving a slip of paper.

'DS Beattie phoned, boss,' he told Knox. 'Found this in Ms Mullen's handbag. Photograph sent as an e-mail attachment. I made a print.'

'Photograph of what?' Knox asked.

'A paper napkin,' McCann said. 'Mark put the call on speaker and I spoke to Liz. She told me the original smells of perfume.'

Knox took the A4 sheet, which bore the likeness of a napkin centred on the page, on the bottom of which was printed: "Summerhall Restaurant and Grill, 207 West Preston Street, Edinburgh".

'Liz says apart from perfume and fold marks, the napkin's almost pristine,' McCann said.

'Recent, then,' Knox said.

'Almost certainly,' McCann said.

Knox held up the paper again. 'No phone number.'

'I checked, boss,' Hathaway said. 'It's in the Yellow Pages.'

'She must have been there sometime on Monday evening,' Knox said. 'Okay, Mark, give the place a ring and see if they can tell you anything.' He paused and added, 'Meantime Arlene and I will head over to Links Place, re-interview Carter. If DI Murray calls, have him ring my mobile.'

'Boss.'

* * *

'The DCI confirmed Bill was given a full suspension?' McCann asked.

Knox brought McCann up to date and few moments later drew to a stop. The detectives were exiting the car when the door to the guest house opened and Mrs Carter came out. She started sweeping the steps and looked up as the detectives approached. 'You're back?' she said.

'Yes,' Knox said. 'We'd like to have another word with your son. He's here?'

She dipped her head in confirmation. 'In the kitchen,' she said. 'Why do you want to see him?'

'Bit of a discrepancy we'd like to clarify.'

'What discrepancy?' Mrs Carter asked.

'I'd prefer to discuss that with him if I may.' Knox pointed towards the door. 'You'll let him know we're here?'

Mrs Carter laid down her broom and called out, 'Willie!'

A few moments later her son arrived at the entrance. He gave Knox a disconcerted look. 'You're here again?'

'Yes,' Knox replied. 'There's somewhere we can talk?'

Carter studied Knox for a long moment, then thumbed in the direction of the hall. 'Aye,' he said. 'The front lounge.'

The detectives followed him inside, where he pointed to chairs near the window. 'You'd better have a seat.'

As his mother made to follow, he turned and gave her a pointed look. 'It's okay, Ma,' he said. 'It's me they want to speak to.'

'You're sure, Willie?'

'Of course I'm sure,' he said sharply.

'Oh,' she said. 'Right, then.' She backed out of the room and added, 'I'll close the door and leave you to it.'

Carter waited until she was back outside and had resumed her sweeping, then took a seat opposite the detectives. 'Ma and I were sorry to hear about Ms Winter's murder,' he said. 'But we told you everything we knew on Monday. Can't imagine there's anything to add.'

'Her backpack,' Knox said. 'We think it strange she took it with her, but left a dressing table full of cosmetics.'

Carter shrugged. 'I said when I spoke to you last. People leave things all the time.'

'What do you do?'

Carter pursed his lips. 'I'm not sure what you mean.'

'With the things people leave behind?'

'Oh, I see,' Carter replied. 'Depends what it is.'

'Something of value, say.'

'We parcel it up and send it on,' Carter said. 'Pay the postage, as a courtesy.' He cleared his throat. 'We've still got Ms Winter's cosmetics. I think Ma put them in a cardboard box… they're in a cupboard somewhere.'

'It's not her cosmetics we're interested in.'

'I already said, she took her backpack with her.'

'Really?'

Carter gave Knox a searching look. 'You're suggesting she left it?'

Knox ignored the question. 'Do you know if Ms Winter had a mobile phone?' he said.

Carter shook his head. 'I never saw her use one.'

'She did,' Knox said. 'An Apple iPhone. On a Canadian network called Trans-Province Utility.' Knox paused and added, 'We asked the company to run a trace on when and where it was last used.'

Carter shifted uncomfortably in his chair but said nothing.

'They've a record of it logging on for just under two minutes at 11.30am on Saturday, 14 March,' Knox went on. 'Links Place, Mr Carter. This exact location.'

A sheen of sweat had formed on Carter's forehead. 'Okay, okay,' he said. 'She left the backpack and her phone was inside. But I switched it on only to check if she'd left a forwarding address. Took a look at numbers listed to see if I might discover anything.'

'And did you?'

'Yes, some in North America, and one from the UK that might've been local. I was going to give it a ring but changed my mind; switched it off again.'

'You had the backpack when we spoke to you on Monday?' McCann said.

Carter gave her a momentary glance and looked at the floor, but said nothing.

'My colleague asked you a question, Mr Carter,' Knox said. 'Did you have the backpack when we spoke to you on Monday?'

Carter continued staring at the floor. 'Yes,' he said. 'Yes, I did.'

'You have it now?' Knox asked.

Carter said nothing.

'When you found out Ms Winter had been murdered, you got rid of it, didn't you?' Knox said. 'What else did it contain? A laptop, an iPod – what?'

'A laptop,' Carter said. 'MacBook Pro.'

'Anything else?'

'Just clothes.'

'The MacBook, you opened it?' McCann asked.

'I took a quick look.'

'At her e-mails?' Knox said.

'Yeah.'

'Inbox and outbox?'

'Both.'

'The ones she received,' McCann said. 'They were from her mother?'

'I think so, yes. Only read a couple of lines.'

'Enough to see that her mother was anxious why her daughter hadn't written?'

Carter shrugged but remained silent.

'You had Ms Winter's phone and her laptop,' Knox said. 'And a means of communicating with her mother, but did nothing. Even though you'd been interviewed by DI Guthrie and knew she was missing?'

'I panicked,' Carter said. 'Thought he'd get the wrong idea, me looking at her stuff.'

'What wrong idea?' Knox asked.

'That I had something to do with her disappearance.'

'And had you?' Knox said.

'Course not.'

'You can see why we'd think it possible,' Knox said. 'With you lying about her backpack.'

'Like I say, I only took a quick look.'

'Who did you sell the mobile and laptop to?' Knox asked.

'I never said I sold it,' Carter protested.

'You didn't have to,' Knox said. 'What did you do with it?'

Carter shifted again, his chair creaking. 'When I read on Monday her body had been found I got the wind up. Flogged them to a guy down the pub.'

'What guy? Which pub?'

Carter shot Knox a hostile look. 'Since you're about to do me for it, that's something I'm not going to tell you.'

'Okay,' Knox said. 'What did you do with the backpack?'

'Dumped it in a skip at a cash and carry.'

Knox held Carter's gaze for a long moment. 'Are you known to us, Mr Carter?'

'Eh?'

'Have you a police record?'

Carter shrugged. 'I did eight weeks in a young offenders when I was sixteen.'

'What for?'

'Breaking and entering.'

Knox mulled this over for a moment, then said, 'You know a man called George Banks?'

'No,' Carter said.

'Okay,' Knox said. 'I'm going to ask another question, and I'd like you to think carefully: did you see the cabbie who brought Ms Winter here?'

Carter thought for a moment or two. 'No, she was standing on the doorstep when I answered the bell. I didn't see a taxi.'

Knox stood. 'You could have saved us a lot of trouble if you'd admitted to having the backpack. And for that reason I'm going to charge you with obstruction. I'm also charging you with its theft, which includes a MacBook laptop and iPhone. You don't need to say anything in answer, but anything you do say will be noted and may be used in evidence. You understand?'

Carter gave Knox a resigned look. 'Aye,' he replied. 'I understand.'

Chapter Fourteen

'Your hunch about the backpack was right, Arlene,' Knox was saying. Ten minutes had passed since he'd spoken to Carter, and the detectives were driving into the Gayfield Square Police Station car park.

'Otherwise he was telling the truth, though,' McCann said. 'He knew nothing about the killer?'

'I originally thought he might be implicated,' Knox said, 'but ruled it out after the second murder.'

'You don't think Carter saw the driver – Banks?'

Knox nodded. 'No,' he said. 'Or whoever dropped her off.'

'You don't think it was Banks?'

'Doesn't fit the description of the man at St Bridget's.'

'So, the tyre prints; unlikely we'll get a match?'

Knox nodded. 'Our best lead to date, but I think we'll draw a blank. Two women, same driver; yet something's amiss.'

'You didn't press Carter on who bought Laura's gear,' McCann said, changing tack.

Knox shrugged. 'Little point. The laptop's hard drive will have been wiped and the mobile's SIM card changed.

In any event I'm confident the killer didn't e-mail or phone either woman – Cassandra Mullen's iPhone proves that.'

Knox parked the car and they climbed the stairs to the office, and were intercepted by Hathaway. 'Finished checking Toyota Prius sales in the Lothians, boss,' he told Knox. 'Popular car. Three main dealers; 439 sales in the last six months alone.'

'Right,' Knox said. 'Not to worry, Mark. I think we've found an easier way to narrow it down.'

Hathaway nodded. 'Oh, and a call came in while you were out. Sam at the front desk switched it through. Guy called Doug Lennie, asked to speak to the officer who arrested Gilliland.'

'What did you tell him?'

'Asked what it was about,' Hathaway said. 'He said he would only speak to the arresting officer. I didn't mention Bill by name, but told him he was out of the office, and might be for some time. Lennie then asked to speak to a supervising officer. I took his number, told him I'd get someone to call him back.' Hathaway took a slip of paper from his desk and handed it to Knox.

Knox glanced at the note. 'A mobile,' he said. 'How long since he rang?'

'About three-quarters of an hour ago. Around 11.30am.'

Knox took out his iPhone and keyed in the number. 'Okay,' he said. 'We'll see what it's about.'

Knox heard three rings, and a voice answered, 'Hello?'

'Doug Lennie?'

'Aye, who's that?'

'DI Jack Knox. You spoke to my colleague in connection with Mr Gilliland's arrest?'

'Oh, aye,' Lennie replied. 'You were the cop who nabbed him?'

'No, that was a colleague of mine, not on duty at the moment.' Knox paused and added, 'What's your connection with Gilliland?'

Lennie's voice dropped an octave. 'Let's just say I know him,' he said. 'Look, I saw the programme with Jackie Lyon on Monday night. She pretty much blamed your mate for Ted's injury. I happen to know he was set up.'

'Sorry, who's Ted?'

'Eddie Gilliland,' Lennie replied. 'His mates call him Ted.'

'I see,' Knox said. 'You said my colleague was set up. How?'

'Look,' Lennie said, his voice hushed. 'I'm at work, can't speak at the moment.'

'Can you call into the office, then?' Knox said. 'Gayfield Square. We can talk here.'

'I'd rather… well, keep it kind of anonymous, like,' Lennie said.

'Where do you want to meet, then?' Knox asked.

'I work–' Lennie cleared his throat and kept his voice low. 'I work in a pub, Rodney Street. Got a break at one o'clock. What about the Waterloo Bar, say quarter past?'

'Okay,' Knox replied.

'Sorry,' Lennie said. 'What did you say your name was?'

'Inspector Jack Knox.'

'Right,' Lennie said, 'see you then, Inspector Knox. Oh, by the way?'

'Yes?'

'You're one of the guys Lyon interviewed?'

'I am.'

'Fine,' Lennie said. 'Just so I recognize you.'

* * *

Lennie, a man in his early forties, had a ruddy face and curly dark hair, and was seated in a corner booth nursing the remains of a pint.

He waved as Knox entered the bar. 'Over here,' he said.

Knox indicated the glass. 'What're you drinking?' he asked.

'Pint of heavy, thanks.'

Knox ordered a half-pint shandy for himself and took both drinks to the table.

'You look different than you do on the telly,' Lennie said as Knox took the seat opposite.

'Really,' Knox replied. 'In what way?'

Lennie shrugged. 'Dunno, a bit taller maybe.'

Knox nodded and changed the subject. 'You said on the phone you had evidence Gilliland's charge against my colleague was false. How come?'

'They were in cahoots, weren't they?' Lennie said.

'Who was?'

'Davie Toomey and Ted.'

'They know each other?'

Lennie snorted into his beer. 'Know each other?' he said. 'Only the best of pals, aren't they?'

'And you know this how?' Knox asked.

'I'm a barman at the Regent Tavern, Inspector Knox,' Lennie replied. 'Have been for over two years. Davie and Ted are regulars. You could say I know them well.'

'They're your mates?'

Lennie took a long pull at his pint, wiped his mouth with the back of his hand, and set the glass back on the table. 'I wouldn't go as far as that. But they're Hearts fans, and I'm a Hibbie. We banter back and forth, indulge in a bit of leg-pulling.' Lennie straightened his glass on a mat and added, 'Thing about being a barman, you get to know the clientele. And hear things.'

'Such as?'

'Such as the fact that Davie's worked for Pik-Pak in Newhaven Road for more than two years, and Ted's been on the dole for six weeks.' Lennie glanced around to make sure no one was within earshot. 'You hear things behind a bar. Particularly after the punters have a few.'

'Go on.'

'Snatches of conversation. Like the fact that Davie's done time for shoplifting, isn't long out of Saughton, sees his probation officer on Wednesdays.'

'What else did you hear?' Knox asked.

'A couple of weeks ago,' Lennie said, 'a lager barrel needed changing. The Regent Tavern's an old-style pub. Access to the cellar is via a trapdoor behind the bar. You've to make sure other bar staff know you're using it — wouldn't want anyone breaking their neck, would you?'

'You wouldn't, no,' Knox agreed.

'Anyways, I make sure the other barmen are aware and go down, switch over the kegs. I'm climbing back up when I hear Ted and Davie talking. Weren't any other staff near because of the open trap, understand?'

'Yes,' Knox replied. 'Carry on.'

'No punters at that end of the bar either, so the two of them talk normal,' Lennie said. 'I hear Davie tell Ted, "The iPhones are kept on a display case at the top of aisle 4, security cord linked to an alarm buzzer. But I'll make sure the one furthest in is disconnected. All you have to do is give it a yank and it'll come free."

'At this point Charlie, the head barman, sees me and says, "Is the new lager keg on, Doug?" Davie and Ted twig I'm there, clam up, and say nothing more. I come up, close the trap, and carry on. Isn't till Monday I'm watching the six-thirty news. Hear Ted's been pinched and injured in the process.'

'You didn't think to bring this to our attention?' Knox said.

Lennie shook his head. 'Like I said, Inspector, in my job I hear all sorts of things. I've learned to treat most with a healthy scepticism. No, I thought nothing more about it till I heard he'd been arrested.'

'Okay,' Knox said. 'You still haven't said how my colleague was set up.'

Lennie took another swig of his beer. 'I was coming to that,' he said. 'Last night Davie comes in with another lad who works at Pik-Pak. A salesman, I think. Bar's busy for a Tuesday – sometimes we get late-night shoppers from Tesco around the corner. They'll stick the groceries in the boots of their cars and drop in for a drink before heading home. Anyhow, I'm serving two old blokes next to Davie, and I hear him blethering to the salesman, who's called Frank. Frank says he'd been interviewed by a cop wanting to know if he saw Ted's arrest.'

'And did he?' Knox asked.

'No. Said he had his back to the aisle where Ted was collared.'

'Right,' Knox said. 'Go on.'

'Yeah, well, at this point one of the old guys at the bar asks for a double and I turn to the optic and pour. My back's to Davie, and even though he drops his voice, I hear him clearly. "Aye, while the older cop was talking to you," he says, "the younger one gave me a nod on the QT, told me they're investigating excessive use of force by the cop who made the arrest."

'"Where were you?" Frank asks Davie.

'"End of the aisle," he says. "This cop thinks the plain-clothes man – an off-duty detective – forced Ted onto a pallet, putting him in hospital. Tips me the wink; didn't I see it happen? I wasn't that close as it happens, but if it puts the arsehole in the shit, I'm happy to oblige."

'Davie laughed. "Who'd've thought it?" he says. "One cop anxious to get another in trouble."'

'You heard Toomey say that?' Knox asked.

Lennie crossed himself. 'Every word,' he said. 'As God's my maker.'

'Did he say anything else?' Knox asked.

'Yes,' Lennie replied. 'The younger cop asked him to repeat the charge in front of his colleague.'

'So the older of the two officers had no part in Toomey's coercion?'

'No. Apparently he'd been talking to Frank at the time.'

Knox thought for a moment. 'You were right, Mr Lennie,' he said. 'What you've told me might make a difference. Would you be prepared to repeat what you've said under oath?'

'Oh, well... I dunno–'

'You told me you saw Ms Lyon's programme on Monday, *Scotland in Focus*?' Knox interrupted.

'I did, yeah.'

'Then you'll know my colleague is facing a serious charge? Gilliland's lawyer intends making the case that he was forced into the pallets and broke a rib, which resulted in a punctured lung. The officers who interviewed Toomey and Frank are from our Professional Standards Department. The charge is a serious one; he has been suspended from duty.'

'I didn't know that,' Lennie said.

'Look,' Knox said. 'I'll speak to Toomey in confidence. I won't mention your name, but say I'm aware he made a false statement. I'll remind him of the gravity of the charge, see if I can get him to change his mind. If that happens, there'll be no need for you to be involved. If he won't, however...'

'I'll need to testify in court?'

'It may not come to that,' Knox said.

'But it might?'

Knox nodded. 'Yes.'

Lennie studied Knox for a long moment. 'Okay,' he said. 'Count me in.'

Chapter Fifteen

He came to, seeing what appeared to be a grey mist; then shapes began to form. Blurred outlines, viewed as through a distorted lens, gradually became sharper.

A man and a woman, dressed in different shades of blue.

The man spoke. 'Mr Doyle?'

Now aware of his surroundings, he saw he lay in bed in a curtained-off cubicle, the cuff of a blood-pressure monitor on the crook of his arm. Feeling a twinge in the back of his hand, he glanced down and saw a cannula inserted into a vein.

'Mr Doyle?' The female, in complete focus, was dark-haired, in her early twenties. She had a slight accent: Scandinavian, possibly German.

'Where am I?'

'You're in the Eastern General Hospital,' the man said. 'I'm Dr Mellor, this is Nurse Beck.'

'What am I doing here?' he said.

'What's the last thing you remember?' Mellor asked.

He racked his brain, trying to recall. Moments later it came back to him: he'd been waiting at traffic lights...

'I was in Hamilton Place,' he said. 'On the way to pick up a fare.'

'You lost consciousness at the wheel of your car, which stalled,' Mellor said. 'Just as well it wasn't travelling at speed.'

'I must've blacked out,' he said. 'What time is it? How long have I been here?'

Beck glanced at her watch. 'One-thirty,' she replied. 'AM. You've been here since ten yesterday morning. Fifteen and a half hours.'

Mellor took a penlight from his pocket. 'I'm going to take a look at your eyes,' he said. 'How are you feeling?'

'Okay, I guess.'

The doctor switched it on and checked the pupils of each eye in turn. 'No grogginess? Nausea?'

Doyle moved his head slightly, following the light. 'No, I don't think so.' He looked directly at Mellor. 'What's wrong with me?' he said.

The doctor indicated the cannula. 'We've taken some bloods, which are currently being tested. We should have the results in the morning. These'll allow us to determine whether it's heart related.'

'You think I've had a heart attack?' Doyle said.

'Not necessarily,' Mellor replied. 'However, it's standard procedure to allow us to determine why you lost consciousness.' The doctor clicked off the penlight, returned it to his pocket, and continued, 'Did you have much to eat before you left home yesterday?'

'Wasn't particularly hungry,' Doyle said. 'I buttered a slice of toast and had it with a cup of tea.'

'Hmm,' Mellor said. 'Low blood sugar's a possibility, as is your blood pressure, which is a bit on the low side. What's more concerning, though, is the length of time you were out.' He paused and added, 'Have you been experiencing any visual disturbances?'

'Sometimes.'

'What exactly?'

'Flashing lights, that sort of thing.'

'In your peripheral vision?'

'At one side of my head, yes.'

'Any fainting spells accompanying these?'

He thought of what had happened when he'd been with Cassie Mullen, but decided to say nothing. 'No,' he said. 'No, I don't think so.'

'I see,' Mellor said. 'Well, we'll do a CAT scan later, just to make sure. It'll mean keeping you in for a couple of days, I'm afraid.' He gestured towards his companion. 'Okay, I'll leave you in the capable hands of Nurse Beck. She needs to get some personal details.'

As Mellor left the cubicle, Beck took a form attached to a clipboard from a nearby table and recorded his full name and address, age and next of kin.

'Any allergies you know of?' she concluded. 'Penicillin, other antibiotics?'

'No, none,' he said.

'You're sure?'

'Yes. I was in the army until recently. Underwent a full medical every year.'

At that moment the monitor at his bedside made a loud series of beeps. The cuff began to inflate, constricting his arm.

Seeing his look of consternation, Beck smiled and said, 'Ambulatory BP reading.'

'Noisy,' he said.

'A bit,' she agreed. 'It's set to take your blood pressure every thirty minutes.'

'Don't know how I remained unconscious all that time with that in my ear.'

She laughed. 'Don't worry, you won't have to endure it much longer. This is an assessment unit. You'll be taken off the monitor when they take you up to a regular ward, later this morning.'

He nodded in acknowledgement, then said, 'Nurse?'

'Yes?'

'Do you know what happened after I blacked out?'

'At the scene, you mean?'

'Yes.'

'The paramedics who brought you in told A&E staff that a couple of motorists waiting behind parked your car at the kerbside. One found a telephone number on the dashboard and rang it. They said a Mr Binks called and picked the car up. Drove it back to your home.'

'Banks,' Doyle corrected. 'My mate, George Banks.'

'Yes, that's correct,' Beck said. 'He inquired at reception. Told him you'd most likely be transferred to a regular ward today. He left a message to tell you he'd call in and see you later.'

Doyle gave an audible sigh of relief. 'That's good to hear, thanks.'

Beck went to end of the cubicle and pulled back the screen. 'Now,' she said, 'I was just going to the staff room to make tea. You'd like a cup; couple of digestives?'

'Yes, please,' he said.

* * *

Knox got into his car, placed his iPhone on the dash mount and keyed in McCann's number, and dialled.

A few moments later he heard her voice, 'Boss?'

'Arlene,' he said. 'Just finished speaking to Lennie. Quite an interesting conversation.'

'It's true?' she said. 'Toomey falsified his statement?'

'Aye,' Knox said. 'But there's more to it than that. Your feelings about DI Simmonds appear more than justified.'

'Really?'

'Yeah. Look, I think we better have a word with Toomey. Drive down and meet me at Pik-Pak in Newhaven Road. I'll go over what Lennie told me when I see you.' A pause. 'Has DI Murray been in touch about Banks's tyre tracks yet?'

'Yes, he called about ten minutes ago. Your hunch was right – no match.'

'I thought so,' Knox said. 'So it's back to the drawing board on that one.'

'Uh-huh,' she said. 'Not sure about forensics on her clothes, though. He's still waiting on DNA results.'

'Right, Arlene, thanks,' Knox said. 'I'm heading to Newhaven Road now.'

'Okay, boss,' McCann said. 'See you there.'

Knox started the car, did a U-turn in Waterloo Place and took the right-hand lane, and turned into Leith Street. The chaos of building the new St James Quarter had improved slightly since the last time he had passed. Its centrepiece – a spiral called the 'Golden Ribbon' – was beginning to take shape and, controversially, starting to rival the twelve-columned National Monument on Calton Hill for the title of 'Edinburgh's Disgrace'.

Knox glanced up and gave a faint smile as he saw the bronzed coil begin to snake its way into the skyline. He now realised why locals had variously dubbed it 'Orange Peel', 'Walnut Whip' and, a lot less flatteringly due to its faecal-like contours, 'Golden Jobby'.

He continued on, and five minutes later pulled into the car park of the Pik-Pak store, where McCann was waiting. Knox exited his car and slid into the passenger seat of her Astra.

After he'd conveyed the gist of his conversation with Lennie, McCann said, 'And Toomey's on duty now?'

Knox glanced at his watch. 'Twenty past four,' he said. 'Collins and Simmonds had to return late on Monday to interview both him and Frank. Lennie tells me he's on the same shift all week.'

McCann dipped her head in acknowledgment. 'How do you think he'll react?'

'Not sure, to be honest,' Knox said. 'All depends what Simmonds said to him.'

'You think the DI warned against changing his statement?'

'Before Collins interviewed him? Yes, I do. Simmonds might have sussed that he and Gilliland were acquainted, that Toomey was in on the theft. It's possible Simmonds brought it up as a way of getting him to go along with the accusation against Fulton.'

'Simmonds would stoop that low?' McCann said.

'You said it yourself, Arlene, you had a feeling about him.'

McCann gave a determined nod. 'Yes I did, didn't I?'

* * *

'A couple of your guys spoke to me late Monday afternoon,' Toomey was saying. 'I told them all I know.'

The shelf-stacker was seated opposite Knox and McCann in a small office in the Pik-Pak warehouse. The manager, Clive Andrews, had allocated the room to the detectives after Knox had requested to see Toomey. Andrews had called his employee to the office and left the detectives to it.

'We're not from the same department as the officers who saw you then,' Knox explained. 'We've called to clarify a couple of details in light of some new information.'

Toomey shrugged. 'Like I say, I told the others all I know.'

'We're not sure you did,' Knox said. 'Had you ever seen Mr Gilliland before?'

Toomey scowled. 'Who told you I had?'

'Just answer the question, please.'

Toomey shook his head. 'No.'

'Really?' Knox said. 'You're not in the habit of drinking with him in the Regent Tavern in Rodney Street?'

Toomey remained silent for a long moment. 'The Regent happens to be my local. If he drinks there, it's a coincidence.'

Knox nodded. 'That's quite plausible,' he said. 'But you've been seen in his company often, haven't you?'

'Whoever said that is lying. I might have bumped into the guy a couple of times, spoken to him in passing, but I don't know him.'

'You're right, Mr Toomey,' Knox said. 'We *have* spoken to someone. Who, naturally, must remain anonymous. But there's a bit more to it than you're saying. Transpires that you and Gilliland are quite pally.'

Toomey's face grew red. 'It's that other cop, isn't it?' he said angrily. 'He told me–'

'Told you what, Mr Toomey?' McCann interrupted.

Toomey gave her a pointed look. 'He was lying to get me to cooperate, wasn't he?'

'You're talking about DI Simmonds?' Knox asked.

'Aye,' Toomey said.

'What did he say to you?'

'Same as you,' Toomey said. 'That I'd been seen with Ted, only he didn't mention where.'

'You admitted you knew Gilliland?' Knox said.

Toomey gave Knox an acerbic look and shrugged. 'Your pal didn't tell you?'

'Tell us what?'

Toomey said nothing.

'You confessed that you and Gilliland had planned the theft?' McCann said.

Toomey made a face. 'He promised there wouldn't be a charge if I kept quiet.'

Knox studied the man for a long moment. 'To answer your question, Mr Toomey: no, DI Simmonds didn't speak to us,' he said. 'Maybe it would be useful if you told us exactly what he said to you.'

'He knew Ted and I were mates,' Toomey replied. 'Said we'd been seen together. Threatened to make inquiries and, if he found proof, he'd throw the book at me.' He shook his head. 'Ted had picked me up at the staff entrance a few times. And you're right, we drank together in the Regent. I knew he was bound to run across someone who'd grass me up.'

'What did you tell him?' Knox said.

'The truth,' Toomey said. 'That I'd put Ted wise to the phone display. Disconnected the alarm of the one he choried. Told him where Benny would be.'

'Benny?' Knox said.

'Benny Wilkie, the security guy,' Toomey replied.

'Go on.'

'Simmonds said CCTV showed me stacking a gondola at the end of the aisle. Asked me to tell him what I saw.'

'Which was?'

'That the plain-clothes cop asked Ted to open the bag, tripped him when he started to leg it.'

'Where did he fall?'

'Into a stack of toasters, at the side of the aisle.'

'He connected with the pallet?'

'Aye.'

'What happened then?'

'Ted got up and tried to run. The cop wrestled him to the ground.'

'Where did the officer arrest him?'

'In the middle of the aisle.'

'Did he use undue force while making the arrest?'

'Sorry, I don't know what you mean.'

'Did he push Gilliland back onto the pallets while handcuffing him?'

'No. He put him in an arm-lock and snapped on the cuffs.'

'You told DI Simmonds this?'

'Aye.'

'What happened then?'

'He suggested that in all the confusion maybe I'd got it wrong, that the cop who made the arrest had been heavy-handed, that when he huckled Ted he'd been a bit over-ze…' Toomey hesitated. 'Sorry, I can't remember the word he used.'

'Over-zealous?' Knox suggested.

'Aye, over-zealous.'

'Go on.'

'That was when he tipped me the wink, like. Said he wouldn't pursue any charge against me if I told his boss that your guy caused Ted's injury. Told me to forget what I actually saw. To say instead that I saw the plain-clothes cop rough up Ted.'

'And did you?' McCann asked. 'Tell DCI Collins that DS Fulton had been instrumental in Gilliland's injury?'

'Yeah,' Toomey said, and gave the detectives a look of despair. 'But I'm still in the doo-dah, aren't I?'

'Your statement to DI Simmonds' senior officer has caused a colleague of ours a lot of trouble,' Knox said. 'He's been suspended for something he didn't do.' Knox looked Toomey in the eye. 'But DI Simmonds is ultimately to blame, not you. He coerced you into making a false statement.'

'Won't make any difference, though, will it?' Toomey said. 'The charge against me won't be dropped?'

'No, it won't,' Knox said. 'However, I can promise I'll make sure what you've told us ensures your case is treated more leniently.'

'What does that mean?' Toomey said.

'Community service as opposed to a custodial sentence,' Knox replied.

'But I'll still lose my job?'

Knox dipped his head in acknowledgement. 'Likely,' he said. 'Better than prison, isn't it?'

'I suppose so,' Toomey said grudgingly.

Chapter Sixteen

Back outside Knox and McCann were standing by their cars when McCann said, 'How are you going to play it, boss?'

Knox glanced at his watch. 'A few minutes after five now. In all likelihood Warburton will have left the office. I'll wait till morning. Give me time to write up reports of our interviews with Lennie and Toomey.'

'He'll speak to Collins?'

'I'm anticipating he will.'

'Collins will want to talk to you.'

'No doubt,' Knox agreed.

'What about Simmonds?'

Knox shrugged. 'He'll try and wriggle out of it, I suppose. Won't wash if I know Collins. Likely he'll find himself at some outpost, shuffling papers.'

'With all the popularity that entails.'

Knox gave a grunt of derision. 'Ex-Complaints? Aye, he's likely to prove very popular.'

'Why, though?' McCann said.

'Why try to stitch-up Bill?' Knox said. 'I've been giving that some thought. You know, Arlene, over the years I've met some chancers in the job. In the minority, but they're there. Men – and, very occasionally, women – who'll do anything to further their careers. Always by unorthodox means, and by being bastards.' Knox paused. 'Simmonds slots into that category.'

Knox pursed his lips and continued, 'I'm of the opinion he made up his mind before he and Collins did Bill's interview. Seeing Jackie Lyon's programme makes him feel justified. So, when the Chief put Bill on ice, he sees a way to score some Brownie points.

'No witnesses? No matter. He quickly susses that Toomey's in bed with Gilliland. Confronts him, is proved right, and decides to bend the facts – intimidates Toomey into falsifying evidence.'

'You're sure Collins will pick up on his motives?' McCann said.

Knox dipped his head in confirmation. 'Like I say, I expect Simmonds to come the innocent, but Collins is shrewd. Like me, he'll have seen more than his share of charlatans. We've two witnesses, don't forget; each independent of the other, and both saying the same thing. No, Collins will recognise it for what it is.'

'Bill's likely to be reinstated soon?'

'In a day or two, perhaps. Better not say anything to him meantime, though. Don't want to tempt fate.'

McCann nodded. 'Yeah, boss,' she said. 'I agree.'

Knox gestured to her Astra. 'Okay,' he said. 'We'll pick it up in the morning. I'm off to the Cowgate. Lucy Carmichael, the pathologist, texted earlier to say she'd have Cassandra Mullen's PM completed by late afternoon. I'll give Mark a ring on the way over, see if there's any updates.'

McCann slid into the driving seat. 'Righto, boss,' she said. 'See you tomorrow.'

As she drove off, Knox got in behind the wheel of his Passat, placed his iPhone on the dash, and dialled Hathaway's number. A moment later he heard the young detective's voice.'

'Hi, Mark,' Knox said. 'Anything cooking?'

'Aye, a couple of things,' Hathaway replied. 'I phoned the Summerhall Restaurant earlier, got the bookings woman, who told me a girl matching Cassandra Mullen's description took dinner on Monday evening with a man matching our confessor. The waiter who served them didn't come on duty until 5pm. I asked her to get him to call me back.'

'And did he?'

'Yes. A Mr Dario Ricci.'

Knox started his car, drove out of the car park, and headed in the direction of the Cowgate. 'Any video?' he asked.

'Aye,' Hathaway replied. 'Mr Ricci sent me an MP4 copy of the CCTV recording via e-mail. Resolution's not that good, as the camera's at the opposite end of the room. Not all that clear on the killer, his back is to the camera.

'They arrived around half eight,' Hathaway continued. 'Stayed just under two hours. Had a meal, general chit-chat. After they finished Mr Ricci approached with the wine list. They declined, had coffee instead. Round about this time she goes to the ladies', comes back to the table after a few minutes. They chat again for a bit, then at twenty past ten he helps her on with her coat and they leave.'

'Mr Ricci say anything else about them?'

'I asked; nothing memorable it seems. She appeared happy enough, they looked to be getting along okay.'

'Right,' Knox said. A beat, and he added, 'You said a *couple* of things.'

'Aye,' Hathaway agreed. 'Arlene told you about the tracks?'

'Yes, no match.'

'Yeah. DI Murray phoned with that just after two. An hour or so later he called back, told me they had forensics on clothing belonging to both women.'

'Anything interesting?'

'Very much so,' Hathaway said. 'They found a hair on Laura Winter's parka, and a skin fragment on the collar of Cassandra Mullen's coat. Mr Murray thinks the latter's a piece of hangnail. Reckon it must have broken off when the killer helped her put on her coat.'

'Okay,' Knox said. 'Don't keep me in suspenders.'

Hathaway gave a little laugh. 'A match, boss. Hair and skin – same DNA.'

'Excellent work,' Knox said. 'I'll need to thank Murray when I next see him.'

'I thanked him on your behalf, boss.'

'Yeah, fine,' Knox said. 'I'll thank him and Liz again anyway. Let them know it's appreciated.' A pause. 'Okay, Mark, you can get off home now. See you in the morning.'

'Okay, boss,' Hathaway said. 'Night.'

* * *

'You just missed Cassandra Mullen's parents,' Lucy Carmichael was saying. The pathologist had just admitted Knox to the Cowgate Mortuary and she and Knox were on their way to the examination room.

'The grief counsellor met them?' Knox said. 'I gave them a ring first thing this morning.'

'Yes,' Carmichael replied. 'Inspector Cox and her assistant were with them throughout.'

'Your text said you'd completed the PM?'

'Yes, before Mr and Mrs Mullen arrived,' Carmichael said. 'Confirms my initial impressions at Blackford Hill.'

They entered the room, where Carmichael went to the examination table and pulled down the sheet covering Cassandra Mullen's body to a fraction below the neckline.

'Cause of death was strangulation,' she continued. 'Almost identical damage to the trachea, like Laura Winter. Similar break to the hyoid bone, too.' She drew the cover down further, exposing the abdomen. Knox saw an I-shaped incision, which had recently been sutured.

'Stomach contents included a partly-digested steak, her last meal,' Carmichael added.

Knox grimaced. 'Mm-hmm,' he said. 'I've just been talking to Mark Hathaway about the restaurant where she ate it.'

Carmichael glanced over and registered Knox's expression. 'You're not comfortable seeing our handiwork?' she said, a mischievous twinkle in her eye.

'Not really,' Knox admitted. 'I attend PMs under sufferance, I'm afraid.'

The pathologist pulled the cover back over the corpse. 'Sorry, Jack,' she said. 'I didn't realise.'

'No, it's okay,' Knox said. 'I've become more or less inured.'

'Okay. Well, as I've said, the PM's complete.' She nodded towards the door. 'Walk me back to the office? I'll make us some coffee and let you have my report before I wind up for the day?'

Knox smiled. 'Sounds fine.'

A few minutes later they were seated in her office, drinking coffee. 'The women's murders, Jack,' she said. 'Any progress on finding the killer?'

'I think so. Forensics have yielded a DNA match with a hair from Laura Winter's parka and a fragment of skin from Cassandra Mullen's coat. Both from the same man, the confessor.'

'The confessor?'

Knox explained about the confession at St Bridget's Church and what they'd discovered about the suspect.

Carmichael shook her head. 'I'm not a psychologist,' she said. 'But I'd guess there's a better than average chance he'll strike again.'

'I know,' Knox said. 'Which is why it's important we nab him soon.'

'You were talking about where she had a meal?'

'Yes,' Knox said. 'After you left Blackford Hill yesterday, we found a restaurant napkin in her handbag;

The Summerhall in West Preston Street. DC Hathaway followed up and obtained CCTV.'

'So you know what he looks like?'

Knox nodded. 'Not the best quality images but, together with the priest and verger's descriptions, a fairly good idea. I've a feeling we're close to a breakthrough.'

They sat in silence for a several moments, then she took a sip of coffee and returned her mug to the table. She studied Knox for a few seconds, and said, 'You were about to ask me something last night… just as your phone rang?'

'Yes,' Knox replied. He cupped his own mug in his hands and looked at her directly. 'I was going to ask you if you'd have dinner with me one evening.'

Carmichael smiled. 'Which evening did you have in mind?'

'What about tonight?'

'When?' she asked. 'I'd need time to change.'

'Your place is nearby, isn't it,' Knox said. 'Jeffrey Street?'

She nodded. 'Yes. But I'd have to freshen up.'

Knox glanced at his watch. 'Yeah, me too,' he said. 'Why don't I drop you off, nip home, and come back and collect you? Almost six now. Say eight-thirty?'

'Okay,' she said, grinning. 'It's a date.'

* * *

Doyle was moved later that morning from the assessment suite to Ward 27, on the second floor. There were three other beds, two of which were occupied. His was nearest the window, which afforded a good view of the nearby Firth of Forth.

After breakfast, a porter called and took him back to the ground floor, where a radiologist performed an MRI scan. He was returned to his ward afterwards and had fallen into a light sleep when he was awoken by someone shaking his elbow. 'Mr Doyle?'

He awoke to see it was Beck, the nurse from the assessment ward. 'Yes?' he said groggily.

'The charge staff tell me you've had your MRI,' she said. 'How are you feeling?'

'Okay, I think,' he replied.

Beck took a chart from the foot of the bed and studied it for a moment. 'I see the results of the blood tests are in,' she said. 'You'll be pleased to learn you haven't had a heart attack, and that your cholesterol count is within normal range.' She placed a thermometer in his ear, checked it, and added, 'Your temperature is okay, too.'

'What about the MRI scan?' he asked.

'We'll have the results later today,' Beck said. 'Dr Mellor will be around to see you then.'

She placed a cuff around his arm and said, 'I'm going to take your blood pressure.' The cuff tightened for a few seconds, then deflated. 'BP still a bit on the low side,' she said. 'But not all that bad.' She undid the Velcro securing the cuff and placed it to one side. 'Okay,' she said, nodding to an ancillary nurse who entered the ward pushing a trolley. 'Time for lunch, then visiting hour at 2pm. I'll call back and see you later this afternoon.'

She made to leave and he said, 'Nurse?'

'Yes, Raymond?'

'You said earlier my mate George left a message. Do you know if he said he'd visit in the afternoon or evening?'

Beck smiled. 'Ah, Mr Banks,' she said. 'I'm sure it was afternoon.'

'Thanks,' Doyle said.

A few moments later the ancillary nurse distributed lunch to him and his two ward-mates, an elderly man and a youth with a bad case of acne.

After the meal, the dishes were in the process of being cleared when the first visitor arrived, a middle-aged woman who went to the old man.

Two others came into the ward seconds later, a man wearing overalls, who headed directly for the youth, and Banks, who had a concerned look on his face.

He approached Doyle and took a bottle of Lucozade from a carrier bag and placed it on his bedside stand. 'Hi, Ray,' he said. 'Feeling better?'

Doyle ignored the question. 'They tell me you picked up the car?'

'Aye,' Banks replied. 'One of the paramedics rang. Said you'd collapsed and had been taken to hospital. What happened?'

Doyle bunched his pillows and leaned towards Banks. 'Had a bit of a turn,' he said. 'Blacked out. They're keeping me in for a couple of days. Observation.' He studied Banks for a moment. 'You look worried – problem with 2Ucabs?'

'No, I gave them a ring. Told them I had a puncture. They'd passed the job on.'

'They were satisfied?'

'Aye,' Banks said. 'There's something else, though.'

'What?'

'Cops. Paid me a visit. Eleven this morning.'

'Cops?'

'Aye. A detective inspector called Knox and his sidekick, a woman.'

'What did they want?' he said. 'Nothing to do with my car?'

Banks shook his head. 'Not that, no. I picked it up. Got your spare key from the plant pot in the garden and garaged it. All secure.'

'What did they want, then?'

'It's to do with the murdered women. The one found at Pathhead and the other at Blackford.'

'Aye, so?'

'Both were picked up by a 2Ucabs driver. The jobs were allocated to our mobile.'

He felt panic rise in his throat but managed to remain calm. 'They've made a mistake, surely?'

'I thought so too. But they told me the 2Ucabs controller verified it with their records. It appears the jobs were accepted when the phone was with you. You don't remember them?'

'Can't say I do.'

Banks shrugged. 'Well, I told them I might have dropped off the woman at Brunstane. Just to keep things okay with 2Ucabs' records. Don't want them finding out about us sharing access. You know it would bugger my contract.'

Doyle shook his head. 'The only thing that connects us – or me, rather – with 2Ucabs is the fact that I picked them up.'

'More than that, Ray. The girl found at Pathhead was taken there by someone in a Toyota Prius; same cars we drive.'

'How do they know that?'

'Tracks were found at the scene.'

Doyle blanched a little. 'They can tell which make of vehicle was used?'

'Apparently. They took my Prius to check. Rang just before I left, let me know I was in the clear. It'll not be back till late afternoon, so I had to get a 2Ucabs here – Stan Logan. Charged me a fiver, enough to cover his petrol.'

'The cops don't know about our arrangement?'

'Of course not,' Banks said, grinning. 'You're not worried they'll check *your* car, are you, Ray?'

Doyle suppressed a sigh of relief. 'No, I'm not. Like you say, wouldn't want to put your contract in jeopardy. It's my living, too.'

'Well, you don't have to worry,' Banks said. 'I made them none the wiser.'

Chapter Seventeen

'I wonder if you'd mind if I asked a personal question?' Lucy Carmichael was saying. She and Knox were seated at a table in a quiet corner of The Witchery Restaurant on Castlehill, where he'd taken her after picking her up at Jeffrey Street.

'No,' Knox said. 'Go ahead.'

'Alex told me you were engaged to be married,' she said. 'That your fiancée, one of the officers in your team, was murdered. Is that true?'

'Yes,' Knox replied. 'Last autumn. By a serial rapist who broke into her flat.'

'Oh my God,' Carmichael said. 'How awful.'

Knox gave a slight nod but said nothing.

'I'm sorry,' she said. 'It was insensitive of me to bring it up.'

'No, it's okay. I'm beginning to come to terms with it.'

The waiter arrived at the table, handed them a menu each, and said, 'Evening, Inspector Knox. How are you today, sir?'

'Fine, Henri. Recommend anything?'

'Isle of Mull scallops starter course is popular this week, sir,' the man said. 'Fillet of halibut with bacon and crème fraîche as a main course.'

'Okay,' Knox said. 'You've sold me.' He glanced at Carmichael. 'Lucy?'

She studied the menu for a moment or two. 'Yes, I'll go with the starter,' she said. 'But I think I might try the chicken. You recommend it?'

'But of course, madam. Stuffed with sweetcorn farce and served with Roscoff onion tart. Delicious. An excellent choice, if I may say so.'

Carmichael smiled. 'Right then,' she said. 'I'll decide on the sweet later.'

The man gave a little bow and said to Knox, 'I'll bring you the wine list in a moment, Inspector.'

'Okay, Henri,' Knox said. 'No hurry.'

As he departed, Carmichael said, 'I take it you're a regular?'

'Don't come in as often as I used to,' Knox replied. 'The staff have a knack of remembering your name. Makes you feel at home.'

'You brought your fiancée here?'

'Yvonne? Yes.' Knox swallowed. 'The last occasion was the day of our engagement.'

Carmichael shook her head. 'There I go again – no bloody subtlety. Sorry.'

Knox smiled. 'No, honestly, I don't mind. None of the team mention her much, sort of dance around the subject any time she's mentioned. Sometimes I think talking about it might help.'

'You're sure?'

'Uh-huh.'

'Okay,' Carmichael said. 'How long were you engaged?'

'Just over a year.'

'Not that long.'

'No.' Knox smiled and shook his head. 'She was eighteen years younger, twenty-nine. Used to tease me that I had a hang-up about our age difference.'

'And did you?'

'I suppose.'

'Forty-seven isn't old.'

'Forty-eight now,' Knox said.

Carmichael smiled. 'I can see why she teased you.'

Knox laughed. 'Aye, you're right,' he said and changed tack. 'Enough about me. What about you?'

'What about me?'

'Your job,' Knox said. 'What made you decide to cut up bodies for a living?'

Carmichael shrugged. 'A route most pathologists take, I guess. After university I spent four years at medical school, during which time the physiology of the human body began to fascinate me.'

'Really?' Knox said, grinning. 'I bet you dissected little animals at school.'

Carmichael laughed. 'How did you guess?' she said. 'No, one of my professors, a woman, really enthused me. She encouraged my interest, and I took a course in pathology at Forth Valley. It lasted three years, after which I qualified.'

The waiter approached at that moment holding a menu and addressed Knox.

'Would you like to order the wine now, Inspector?' he said.

'I'm driving, Henri,' Knox said. 'So only beer for me, please. Pint of lager shandy. Light on the lager.'

'Pint of lager shandy, two-thirds lemonade, sir.' He turned and gave the menu to Carmichael. 'And the lady?'

She scanned the wine list for several moments, then gave the waiter a querying look. 'I'm not really sure. What do you recommend?'

'The sauvignon blanc is excellent, madam,' he said. 'Two-year-old New Zealand, an excellent wine.'

'Okay,' Carmichael said. 'I'll go with that. A demi bottle, please.'

'Certainly, madam. Thank you.' He retrieved the menu, tucked it under his arm, and moved off just as a commis waiter set down their starters.

Knox scooped out one of the scallops, finished eating it, and said, 'So, why Dundee?'

'You mean after I completed the pathology course?'

Knox nodded. 'Yes.'

'I heard of an opening with the Central's team, applied, and was accepted. That was fourteen years ago.'

'You're not from Dundee, though?'

Carmichael smiled. Can't hide my west of Scotland accent, eh?' she said. 'No, Glasgow. Pollokshields to be exact.'

'What made you relocate to Edinburgh?'

'From Dundee?' Carmichael said. 'A colleague and friend of mine, a doctor, moved to the city four years ago. Invited me to stay at her New Town flat weekends and holidays. I fell in love with the place's cosmopolitan atmosphere. Probably helped, too, that I spent my last break here during last year's festival.'

'Did you take in many shows?'

'That'd be a hard job,' Carmichael said. 'So much going on, isn't there? I caught one or two of the Fringe offerings and went to the Lyceum theatre. Saw Wilde's *The Importance of Being Earnest.*'

Knox grinned, put on a falsetto voice and gave his best Lady Bracknell impression: 'A *hand*-bag?'

Carmichael laughed. 'Hey, that's very good,' she said. 'No, not with Dame Edith Evans, but a great production.'

Knox shook his head. 'You know, it's a fact most locals never see much of what's on at festival time, and that includes me. Though my son Jamie came over last year with his wife and my granddaughter. We went to the Tattoo and thoroughly enjoyed it.'

Carmichael nodded. 'Yes,' she said. 'Quite a spectacle, isn't it?'

'Aye. Takes some beating.'

They had finished the starter when the waiter returned and placed Knox's shandy on a coaster, uncorked a half-bottle of sauvignon blanc, and poured a little into Carmichael's glass.

She took a sip and nodded approvingly. 'Excellent,' she said. 'Very nice wine. Thank you.'

The man half-filled her glass, placed the bottle on the table in front of her, gave a little nod and said, 'Thank *you*, madam.'

'So,' Knox said as the waiter departed, 'Alex told me he'd be retiring sometime this year but didn't say when. Any idea when you'll be taking over?'

'August or September, I think,' Carmichael said. 'It'll give me time to settle in.' She took another sip of wine. 'He won't be retiring fully for another year or so, though.' She smiled. 'Tells me he wants to wind down slowly.'

They eat in silence for a minute or two, then Knox said, 'My turn to risk a charge of insensitivity. We've already talked about the pressures of work. Have you any regrets that it may have cost your marriage?'

'Sometimes,' she said. 'You?'

Knox dipped his head in reply. 'I'd be lying if I said otherwise.'

'Did you and your wife ever consider getting back together?'

'Not really,' he said, then shrugged. 'In any event, she moved to Australia soon afterward, by which time…'

'You'd met Yvonne?'

'Yes,' Knox said.

'George,' Carmichael said, 'my husband, tried to repair the damage when I discovered he was cheating.' She shrugged. 'But I shut him out. Ego, I guess. Just couldn't handle it.'

As Knox acknowledged this his mobile rang. He glanced at the screen and saw it was Fulton. 'Excuse me while I take this,' he said. 'A colleague.'

'Of course,' Carmichael replied.

'Bill?' Knox said.

'Sorry to call so late, boss,' his sergeant said. 'Just spoke to Mark. Tells me you interviewed a guy called Lennie. Simmonds is trying to pull a fast one?'

Knox shook his head. 'I'd hoped to keep it under wraps till tomorrow, Bill. Didn't want to get your hopes up.'

'It's true, though?' Fulton said. 'The guy interviewed at Pik-Pak gave a false statement?'

'Looks that way,' Knox replied. 'I intend taking it up with Warburton in the morning. Like I say, didn't want to get in touch till I was sure.' He paused. 'Hadn't reckoned on Mark jumping the gun.'

'He didn't, boss,' Fulton said. 'I called him and managed to wheedle it out of him.'

'Ah, right,' Knox said. 'Okay, I'll give you a ring after I speak to Warburton. Wee bit of luck we'll have you back within twenty-four hours.'

'Great news, boss. Thanks.'

'Don't go thanking me yet,' Knox said. 'Still a couple of hoops to jump through. Have to convince Collins that his partner's gone rogue.'

'I know, boss. I know.'

'Okay, Bill. Speak to you tomorrow.' Knox rang off and returned the mobile to his pocket.

'DS Fulton?' Carmichael asked.

'Yes.'

'To do with the injury to the thief he arrested?'

'Uh-huh,' Knox replied. 'Some interdepartmental chicanery at work. Something I hope to be able to resolve.'

'It'll clear DS Fulton?'

'I hope so.'

They continued chatting though dinner, after which Knox called for the check, settled the bill, and left a tip. They exited the restaurant and drove the short distance back to Jeffrey Street.

Knox parked outside her flat and Carmichael turned to face him. 'Thanks for dinner, Jack,' she said. 'I thoroughly enjoyed it.'

Knox smiled. 'You're welcome.'

As she leaned over and pecked his cheek, he pulled her towards him and kissed her fully on the lips. She pulled away suddenly and said, 'No, Jack… please don't.'

Knox looked surprised. 'But I thought you…'

She shook her head. 'I've had a delightful evening, Jack, really I have. Sorry if I gave the wrong impression.'

'It's my fault,' Knox said. 'I just assumed that you were…'

'Ready for another relationship? Yes, apparently so did I. My husband's affair seems to have affected me more than I thought.' She paused and added, 'I like you, Jack, really I do.'

Knox smiled. 'It's okay,' he said. 'No damage done.' Then quickly added, 'Except maybe a little bruising to my ego.'

She reached over and touched his arm. 'No, Jack. It's not you. It's just that I…'

'Need a little more time?' Knox volunteered.

'I think so, yes. You'll forgive me?'

Knox shook his head. 'Nothing to forgive, Lucy.' He paused. 'Hurt sometimes takes longer to heal than we realise.'

Chapter Eighteen

Banks and the other visitors hadn't been gone long when Dr Mellor entered the ward, accompanied by a younger man Doyle took to be a junior medic. The pair walked over and Mellor drew the curtain screening the bed.

'Good afternoon, Raymond,' he said. 'How are you today?'

Doyle looked at the doctor with a degree of apprehension. 'I think you're better qualified to tell me that,' he said.

Mellor grinned. 'Quite,' he said and waved to his companion. 'This is Dr Singh. Dr Singh's recently joined our staff and is doing the rounds with me today. You've no objection to me discussing your diagnosis and treatment in his presence?'

Doyle shook his head. 'No, none.'

'Good,' Mellor said, then glanced at his notes. 'Well, we've received the results of your MRI scan and I'm happy to tell you it reveals nothing untoward.' He paused and looked at his notes again. 'Tell me, Raymond, have you been sleeping okay?'

'I think so,' Doyle replied.

'How many hours on average would you say?'

'Six or seven.'

'And you work as a taxi driver?'

'Yes.'

'Mostly in town?'

'Yes.'

'Mm-hmm,' Mellor said. 'Driving in traffic all day can be very stressful. You have to make sure you get adequate sleep. Then there's the question of diet. You told me in the assessment ward that you had very little to eat when you left home on Tuesday morning. I explained then that low blood sugar could be a factor. You should be aiming for a proper breakfast; most important meal of the day. I'm more concerned about your blood pressure, however, which is still a tad on the low side: 93 over 63 currently, 89 over 60 when you were admitted.'

Doyle shook his head. 'Sorry, Doc,' he said. 'I don't know what that means.'

'One of the effects of low blood pressure,' Mellor explained, 'is syncope, which results in blurred vision and fainting, a couple of the symptoms you've experienced. Possibly exacerbated in your case by stress, and perhaps low blood sugar. Nothing to worry about though; I'm going to prescribe a short course of fludrocortisone tablets, which you'll take over the next month. I'll send your GP a note to check your blood pressure again then and decide whether to keep you on them longer.'

'That's what was causing flashes in my vision?' Doyle asked.

Mellor nodded. 'I think so,' he said. 'Your blackout too, most likely.'

Images of Laura Winter and Cassie Mullen flashed through his mind, and for a moment he thought of asking about the possibility of possession while in a state of unconsciousness. But he thought better of it and said nothing.

'We'll discharge you early tomorrow,' Mellor concluded. 'If you commence taking the tablets you should be okay. Have you any questions?'

'No, Doc,' Doyle replied. 'You've explained everything. Thanks.'

* * *

The following morning he returned to see a Toyota Prius parked outside his house. As he paid off the taxi, Banks exited his driveway and walked over. 'Ray,' he said. 'So they *did* discharge you. Expected they would. What was wrong?'

'Low blood pressure,' Doyle replied. 'Got me on a course of tablets, haven't they?' He thumbed towards his garage. 'You were leaving the mobile?'

'Aye,' Banks said. 'Wasn't sure whether to or not. Thought you'd be taking a day or two off.'

'Can't afford it: car repayments.'

'Aye, I suppose,' Banks said. 'Okay, Ray, I'm away to get some kip. Been a busy shift.'

'What's it like now?'

Banks opened his car door and made to enter. 'Ticking over,' he replied. 'Quite a few jobs in the city centre.' He slid into the driver's seat and added, 'See you later.'

'Right, George, I'll get to it,' Doyle replied. 'See you.'

He went to his garage, backed his Prius into the street, and opened the glove box and took out the iPhone. A click on 2Ucabs' icon told him of two jobs waiting, both equidistant: one in George Street and the other in Leith. He selected the one in George Street and was allocated the fare: a couple called Perry waiting at The George Hotel.

As he drove off, he thought about his predicament, and came to the conclusion it was only a matter of time before the cops discovered his arrangement with Banks. Once that happened, it was inevitable they'd run a test on his tyres, which would result in a match with the prints on their files.

A risk he couldn't afford to take.

The job at The George Hotel was only a short one: from the hotel to Jenners in Princes Street. Once he'd dropped them off, he'd take a five-minute drive to Kwik Fit at McDonald Road and have them change all four. He was lucky that when he had taken delivery of the Prius, he'd asked the dealer to fit winter-spec Michelins. Although they were good for a few thousand miles yet, it was Spring, and switching them shouldn't arouse suspicion.

What did that leave? He'd picked up both women; no way around that. A fact which proved nothing, however. When it came right down to it, they could have met their murderer anywhere.

Anything else? CCTV was likely, but he could think of only two places that might put him in danger: St Bridget's Church, and the restaurant where he'd taken Cassie Mullen.

He'd driven up and down Bonnington Road at least a half-dozen times in the last few days, and only at the Leith end had he seen cameras – those mostly covering an industrial estate.

What about the church itself? He didn't think so. He'd taken note in both the vestibule and nave and hadn't seen any.

Which left the restaurant. He'd been a customer three or four times prior to Monday, and could recall only one camera near the kitchen entrance. If he remembered correctly, that particular unit was positioned facing the door, and as such would have had a view of his back, which wouldn't allow police to make a positive ID.

What did that leave?

Well, at some point he could have transferred his DNA. Again, he thought it unlikely. He was scrupulous about his car, vacuuming the interior and cleaning all surfaces at the end of each shift. He didn't think anything could have been picked up that might incriminate him.

Which left skin-to-skin contact. He read that DNA could be transferred from one person's skin to another.

Just as well, then, he'd had the presence of mind to rub the hands and necks of both women with antibacterial wipes he carried in the glove box. He concluded that there was nothing to worry about. If the cops came calling all he had to do was keep calm and hold his nerve.

A few minutes later he arrived at George Street and stopped outside the hotel. No one was waiting, so he got out of the car and made for the entrance. As he did so, he caught the attention of a roving traffic warden, who approached, ticket book in hand.

Doyle nodded towards the hotel entrance. 'Picking up a fare,' he said. 'Won't be a minute.'

'Better not be longer,' the man said sternly. 'Else I'll issue you with a ticket.'

Two women in their early twenties exited at that moment, a blonde and a brunette. The latter looked in Doyle's direction and said, '2Ucabs?'

'Yes, madam,' Doyle replied. 'You're Ms Perry?'

The woman indicated her companion. 'She's Perry,' she said in an American accent. 'I'm Baker.' She gave a little laugh. 'Angie and Janice, if you want to be less formal.'

'You're going to Jenners?' he said.

'Yeah,' the blonde said. 'That's a department store, right?'

'Yes, madam.' Doyle opened the rear passenger door and waved them inside. The warden gave a look of disappointment as Doyle slid into the driver's seat, put the Prius into gear, and moved off.

The brunette clicked her seatbelt into place and said, 'Angie wants to go shopping. But I'd prefer to do some sightseeing. The concierge told us city tours leave from Waverley Bridge. That's near the store?'

'Almost opposite, madam,' Doyle said.

'There're coaches?'

'Yes, madam. Quite a few to choose from. All operate from Waverley Bridge.'

A short pause, and she added, 'I don't suppose *you* do city tours?'

Doyle's interest was immediately piqued. The fare from The George Hotel to Jenners was £3.80. A city tour on the other hand…

'Yes, madam,' he said enthusiastically. 'I certainly do.'

He glanced in the mirror and saw the brunette turn to her friend. 'What do you say, Angie?' she said. 'Give you all morning to exercise your plastic. Meet me back at The George for lunch?'

The woman gave an insouciant shrug. 'Whatever,' she said.

The brunette caught Doyle's eye, and smiled. 'Okay, we'll drop Angie at the store. You can show me the sights.'

'Certainly, madam,' he said.

'Right,' she said. 'And you can cut the madam. My name's Janice.'

Chapter Nineteen

'This Douglas Lennie,' Warburton was saying. 'He's willing to swear under oath?'

Knox was in his boss's office going over his conversation with the barman and the subsequent interview with Toomey.

'Yes, sir,' Knox confirmed. 'He assured me he was.'

'H-mmm,' Warburton said. 'And you're confident about the shelf-stacker?'

'Yes, sir. His testimony was witnessed by DS McCann, and is as exactly as in my report.'

The DCI shook his head. 'Well, I've encountered some damnable things in my time, but this takes the biscuit.' He glanced at Knox's report again. 'What the hell does Simmonds hope to achieve?'

'To curry favour at HQ?' Knox suggested. 'Jackie Lyon's programme put the force under a fair bit of pressure regarding brutality charges, particularly since the issue's been aired in parliament.'

'By encouraging a false statement to the detriment of a fellow officer?' Warburton shook his head and added, 'Beggars belief.'

'But not without precedent, sir.'

'I know,' Warburton said. He straightened in his chair. 'Very well, I'll get in touch with DCI Collins. Simmonds may be a rotten apple, but I've every confidence in his boss. We go back a long way. I assure you he'll take a particularly dim view of this.'

'Yes, sir,' Knox said. 'I know him from St Leonards. I have that impression, too.'

'Right,' Warburton said. 'I'm told he's at St Leonards all week. I'll get in touch, arrange for you and McCann to see him later today.' A pause. 'You do realise DI Simmonds will be there, too?'

'I do, sir.'

'Okay, Jack. Leave it with me.'

Knox exited Warburton's office and joined McCann and Hathaway, who were seated at their desks. He relayed the gist of his conversation with the DCI, and McCann said, 'You don't think Simmonds'll put his hands up?'

'Mea culpa?' Knox replied. 'Unlikely. Not to worry, Arlene,' he added. 'Worm on a hook. As I said yesterday, can't see him wriggling his way out of this one.'

Knox strode to the whiteboard. 'Okay, that's for later.'

He turned and tapped the surface with a marker. 'Meanwhile let's concern ourselves with the confessor. I've marked the board with the latest information; DNA from hair and skin samples. The moment a suspect is nabbed, we'll know if he's our man.' He thumbed to the board and faced the detectives. 'Any theories?'

'Yeah, boss,' Hathaway said. 'I've one.'

'Let's hear it,' Knox replied.

'George Banks.'

'What about him?'

'He picked up the women, yet his tyre tracks were negative. Which means it couldn't have been his car at Pathhead.'

'Yes, I know,' Knox said. 'So?'

'But it's likely to have been a Toyota Prius, same model Banks drives?'

'Agreed,' Knox said. 'Go on.'

'I've a mate in the taxi trade, boss. Black cab owner. Runs a new TX model. Those cars aren't cheap, around fifty-six grand. Has to be worked 24/7 in order to make it pay. It's double-shifted. My mate works nights, has another driver on days.'

'And your point is?' Knox said.

'A Toyota Prius isn't anywhere near as expensive,' Hathaway replied. 'Even with running costs – particularly if it's being driven by the owner driver.' He nodded towards McCann. 'Arlene said when you and she arrived to interview him at 11am, Banks was wearing a dressing gown. Made me curious. I rang 2Ucabs. Turns out he regularly signs on around 10pm, works until 4am. Typically he'll start again around 10am. Work till five or six in the evening. I'm wondering if he's actually working all those hours.'

'That's right, boss,' McCann said. 'Took him a while to come to the door. Looked like he was just out of his kip.'

'Which got me thinking,' Hathaway continued. 'What if he's somehow passing on work to someone else — someone who, like him, runs a Toyota Prius?'

Knox thought for a moment or two, and the truth dawned. 'You're right, Mark,' he said. 'But he's not just passing on work — he's passing on the phone.'

'Of course,' McCann agreed. 'He told us 2Ucabs operators get their business via an app on their smartphones—'

'Which are unique to each operator,' Knox interrupted. 'Banks didn't accept the jobs and pick up the women. Whoever was using his phone did.'

'I don't understand, though,' Hathaway confessed. 'Why didn't the guy have an app on his own phone?'

'Because 2Ucabs wouldn't issue him with one,' Knox said. 'Your mate with the black cab is licenced through the Cab Office, which we oversee. Anyone who applies to operate a taxi is checked to make sure they've a clean sheet. If they've a record — for assault or something similar — they'll be turned down. Private hire companies like 2Ucabs must abide by the same rules.'

Hathaway gave a nod of comprehension. 'Which Banks is allowing him to get around. I wonder why?'

'Only one way to answer that,' Knox said. 'Arlene and I will have to pay him another visit.' He indicated the phone on Hathaway's desk, and added, 'Get back on to 2Ucabs again, Mark. Find out when Banks signed off this morning. You can update us on our way there.'

* * *

Knox was turning into Logie Green Road when his dash-mounted iPhone rang. He slowed the Passat to a crawl, keyed the *accept call* icon, and said, 'Mark?'

'Just off the phone with 2Ucabs, boss,' Hathaway said. 'Banks accepted a job at 4.22 this morning. Grange Loan to the airport.'

'Anything after that?'

'No activity on his mobile from then until five minutes ago.'

Knox checked his watch and saw it was approaching ten. 'Until 9.55am? What happened then?'

'The controller told me he just claimed another fare in the city centre. George Hotel to Jenners.'

Knox continued along Logie Green Road and McCann nudged his elbow. 'Isn't that his Prius parked outside his flat?' she said.

Knox pulled in behind the Toyota, took a notebook from his pocket, and leafed through it until he found the page he was looking for. 'Yes,' he said. 'Same registration. It's Banks's car all right.'

There was a hum of static and Hathaway's voice came over the speakers again. 'Did you get that, boss?' he said.

'Loud and clear, Mark,' Knox said. 'Arlene and I were checking a discrepancy.'

'Discrepancy?' Hathaway said.

'Aye,' Knox replied. 'Banks appears to be in two places at once.'

'His car's there?' Hathaway said.

'Very much so,' Knox confirmed. 'Looks like your theory's correct.' He switched off the ignition and set the Passat's handbrake. 'Look, Mark, keep in touch with the 2Ucabs controller, will you? I want to know if Banks's doppelganger claims any other jobs, and where he's headed if he does.'

'Right, boss. I'll get right on it.'

The detectives exited the car, went to the entrance to Banks's block, where Knox thumbed the intercom.

A moment or two later they heard a voice. 'Yeah?'

'Mr Banks?' Knox said. 'It's Detective Inspector Knox and Detective Sergeant McCann. We spoke yesterday.'

'Aye? Your guys checked the car, told me they were satisfied when they dropped it off. What's it this time?'

'Yes, as you say, the car's been cleared. No, it's something else. May we speak to you, please?'

A short silence. 'Aye, I suppose,' Banks said, and the buzzer sounded. 'Come on up.'

Banks was wearing the same blue pyjamas and checked dressing gown when they arrived at the third floor. He ushered them into the living room, indicated the settee and again took a seat next to the dining table. 'Thought we covered everything when I spoke to you last.'

'Not quite,' Knox replied.

'I don't understand,' Banks said.

'A question relating to the laws of physics,' Knox said.

'Eh?' Banks replied, a dumbfounded look on his face.

'Aye,' Knox said. 'How someone can be in two places at the same time.'

Banks's face paled. 'I'm not with you,' he said.

'Oh, you're with me all right, Mr Banks,' Knox said. 'But I don't think your phone is.'

'M-my phone?'

'Yes, the smartphone you use exclusively for your 2Ucabs work. The one with their app.'

Banks studied Knox for several moments, then said, 'Who told you about Ray? The hospital?'

Knox returned his gaze. 'No, they didn't,' he said, and added, 'Perhaps you would like to explain.'

'About the hospital?'

'No, about Ray,' Knox said. 'You can tell us about the hospital afterwards.'

Banks shook his head. 'Maybe I shouldn't have agreed to it,' he said. 'But we're old mates. Served in the army together, Royal Logistics Corps.'

'Before we start,' Knox said. 'You'd better tell us who you're talking about.'

'You mean Ray?'

'Yes,' Knox replied, taking out his notebook. 'What's his full name?'

'Raymond Doyle.'

'Address?'

'Twenty-one Redbraes Crescent.'

'Age?'

'A couple of years younger than me, I think. Twenty-seven.'

Knox wrote this down. 'Okay,' he said. 'You were explaining how this arrangement with 2Ucabs came about?'

'Aye, like I say, we're mates, in the army together. Finished our stint the same time. Palled up again in civvy street. He was working as a long-distance lorry driver then, but getting fed up with it. I started with private hire after I was demobbed and told him about it. He fancied giving it a try, completed the paperwork. A week or two later got the news that he'd been turned down.'

'Why, did he say?' McCann asked.

'Yeah, at sixteen he'd been charged with having sex with a girl a couple of years younger. Apparently she'd led him on, afterwards claimed he'd raped her.'

'So you came to an arrangement to share your phone?' Knox said.

'Well, I'd recommended the job, hadn't I?' Banks retorted. 'And by then he'd quit his and leased a new Toyota Prius.' A pause. 'I felt responsible.'

'I take it 2Ucabs know nothing about this?'

'No, it's against their rules.' Banks shrugged. 'What else could I do? Leave him high and dry?' Banks paused for a moment, and added, 'Anyway, it suits us both. I like working nights, Ray prefers days.'

'He began driving taxis with you two years ago?' McCann asked.

'Yeah.'

'You said he drives a Toyota Prius,' Knox said. 'Do you happen to know its registration number?'

Banks shook his head. 'No, sorry. Only that he got it last year.'

'You mentioned a hospital?'

'Yeah. Ray collapsed while on his way to pick up a fare in Stockbridge on Tuesday. Fortunately, he was sitting at traffic lights in Hamilton Place at the time.'

'Which hospital was he taken to?' Knox asked.

'Eastern General,' Banks replied. 'Kept him in for a couple of days and ran some tests. Told me they put him on pills for blood pressure.'

'He was released this morning?'

'Yeah. I was dropping off the phone at his garage when he arrived back.'

'That's a habit?' McCann said. 'You take the mobile to him at the end of your shift?'

'Yeah, I finish early doors. I've a key to his garage. Stick the mobile in the glove box to avoid disturbing him. He's got one of my spare keys, does the same for me.'

'You've spoken to him lately?' Knox asked.

'When I handed over the phone, yeah.'

'You told him your car had been examined?'

'Not this morning. I mentioned it when I visited him in hospital, though. Yesterday.'

'How did he react?' McCann said.

Banks raised his eyebrows. 'Wait a minute,' he said. 'You checked my car in connection with the murders. You're telling me now that you suspect Ray?'

McCann said nothing.

'You haven't answered my colleague's question,' Knox said. 'How did he react when you told him your car had been impounded?'

'He was taken aback a bit,' Banks replied. 'When I joked about him being a suspect, he assured me his only concern was 2Ucabs discovering our arrangement.' He paused, a look of concern on his face. 'It *is* Ray, isn't it? Jesus! I never thought that for a minute. You've got to believe me.'

He gave Knox a searching look, and added, 'Am I in trouble? Do I need a lawyer?'

'You could have saved us a lot of bother if you'd told us about Doyle earlier,' Knox replied. 'But I believe you kept quiet because of your contract with 2Ucabs.'

Knox closed his notebook and he and McCann rose. 'For that reason, I won't bring a charge of obstruction, so your immediate problems are with them. If you contact Doyle after we go, however, or warn him if he gets in touch, that'll change. You understand?'

'Yeah, yeah, of course,' Banks said meekly. 'You have my word.'

Chapter Twenty

Once the detectives were back in the car, Knox rang Hathaway, gave him a précis of Banks's interview, and asked, 'You checked with 2Ucabs? Doyle hasn't claimed any other work?'

'No, I guessed it would only be a ten-minute trip to Jenners,' Hathaway replied. 'So I waited till ten-thirty and called back. They confirmed the department store trip was the last job allocated, and that there were still a few fares in the area. The controller, a Ms Randall, thought it was unusual he hadn't put in for one. Said she would call The George Hotel to check and get back to me.'

'And did she?' Knox asked.

'Aye, fifteen minutes ago, just before eleven,' Hathaway replied. 'The concierge told her two Americans had phoned for the cab, Ms Angela Perry and Ms Janice Baker. Perry had just arrived back at the hotel when Randall phoned. The concierge spoke to her, who told him her friend had held on to the cab, asked the driver to take her on a city tour.'

'She's still with Doyle?' Knox asked.

'It would appear so. Ms Perry said they'd arranged to meet back at The George for lunch.'

'How old is Ms Baker?'

'The concierge reckons in her mid-twenties.'

'Right, Mark,' Knox said. 'We've got to find Doyle, and quick. Get on to the DVLA and get his index number. Once you have it, put out an alert for both Traffic and patrol vehicles: stop and apprehend. If it's a city tour, he's in the Edinburgh area. With a bit of luck, we'll run him down quickly.'

'Boss,' Hathaway said. A brief pause, and Knox heard his voice again. 'Oh, and boss?'

'Yes?' Knox said.

'Another call came in just before you phoned. DCI Collins. Wanted you to drop in at St Leonards and see him around noon. To do with DS Fulton's alleged assault on Gilliland.'

'What'd you tell him?'

'That you were close to collaring a murder suspect. That it might delay you.'

'Good call, Mark. That meeting will have to be back-burnered. What did he say?'

'That he understood the case took precedence. Told me he and DI Simmonds would be at St Leonards all day. Said you could call in later.'

* * *

He began at the foot of the Royal Mile. Baker sat beside him in the front passenger seat, and insisted on calling him Ray.

He drove into Abbey Strand where the gates to Holyrood Palace were closed. 'They're only open when the Queen's in residence,' he explained.

'Odd name, Holyrood,' she said.

Doyle pointed to a ruin beside the palace. 'Has its origins in the Abbey,' he told her, 'which was built by David I in 1128. Apparently, he was hunting a stag in the park when the animal attacked, pinning his thigh to the ground. When he grabbed its antlers, they turned into a crucifix, after which the animal bolted.'

She pointed to the hill beyond. 'The park over there?'

'Holyrood Park, yes,' Doyle replied. 'Adjacent to the Palace.'

'Ah,' she said. 'Sorry, Ray. Carry on.'

'Well,' Doyle continued, 'legend has it he had a dream in which he was told to make a house devoted to the cross. He built the Abbey and named it the Monastery of the Holy Rood.'

Baker gave a low whistle. 'Amazing,' she said, then pointed to Holyroodhouse. 'That's much later, of course?'

He nodded. 'Built between 1528 and 1532. The south-west tower by Robert Mylne was added between 1671 and 1676.'

'Where the Queen lives?'

'Only when she's in Scotland. Usually in June.'

'When she hosts garden parties, right?'

'Yes,' he agreed.

'Ever get an invite?'

'Not yet,' he said, grinning. 'Maybe one of these days.'

He turned the car and drove up the Royal Mile, pointing out White Horse Close, where Mary, Queen of Scots stabled her favourite mount, a white palfrey.

'Didn't I also read that the place has a connection with Bonnie Prince Charlie?' Baker asked.

'Yes, you're right,' he replied. 'Many of the Highland chiefs and officers were quartered there during the 1745 Jacobite uprising.' He turned to her and added, 'You know your Scottish history.'

'Yeah,' she replied. 'My great-uncle Donald hails from Dunfermline in Fife. I've been steeped in it since I was a kid.'

'He's still living, your great-uncle?'

'Yeah. Eighty-four. Hail and hearty.'

Doyle next stopped at Canongate Kirk, where Baker pointed to a bronze figure situated outside the gate. 'Who's that a statue of?' she asked.

'Robert Fergusson, the poet.'

'Yeah, I seem to recall Donald mentioning him,' Baker said. 'Didn't he influence Robert Burns?'

'Yes,' Doyle replied. 'He was only twenty-four when he died. Burns discovered he'd been buried in an unmarked grave and commissioned a headstone. Paid for a fenced-off plot.'

'In this churchyard?' Baker asked.

'Yes.'

Baker nodded. 'I must get around to visiting it sometime.'

'Are you and your friend in Edinburgh long?'

'Only a couple of days. Business. We're getting a train to Inverness tomorrow. Meeting some of our suppliers.'

'Oh,' Doyle said. 'What line of business are you in?'

'Clothing,' Baker replied. 'Knitwear, to be more specific. We specialise in sweaters, scarves, that sort of thing.'

'Where in the US are you based?'

'Syracuse. New York State.'

Doyle nodded acknowledgement and carried on up the Royal Mile, pointing out places of interest en route, and came to the Netherbow, where the cobbled street narrowed to accommodate one of the oldest buildings in the High Street, a mediaeval property dating from the

1500s, former home of firebrand Protestant cleric, John Knox.

'Jeez,' Baker said. 'Amazing how it's survived, creating a sort of bottleneck. In the States it would've been razed years ago.'

'It's a listed building,' Doyle explained. 'An important part of Scotland's heritage.'

'Oh, I know,' Baker said. 'To do such a thing would have been sacrilege.' She pointed to the structure and continued, 'He was a character, though, wasn't he? Didn't like to see females in a position of power. Donald told me he put out a pamphlet about it. Is that true?'

'Yes, entitled *The First Blast of the Trumpet Against the Monstrous Regiment of Women*,' Doyle replied. 'Said to have been aimed at Mary, Queen of Scots and her cousin, Queen Elizabeth. He tried to persuade Mary to give up the Catholic faith, but she refused. She found him quite intimidating, apparently. Quoted as saying, "I fear Knox's prayers more than the assembled armies of Europe."'

Baker smiled. 'Religion and politics, eh? An explosive mix.'

'Yes,' Doyle agreed. 'Highly combustible.'

He ended the tour, where he had begun it with Mullen three days earlier, at the Castle Esplanade, and again highlighted the view across Princes Street and the New Town.

Baker pointed towards the Firth of Forth. 'Other side of the estuary there,' she said. 'That's Fife?'

'Yes,' Doyle agreed. 'We're lucky with the weather. The stretch of coast you can see lies between Burntisland and Aberdour.'

'And Donald's birthplace, Dunfermline?'

'More to the left, further inland.'

She glanced at her watch. 'I guess a trip there will have to wait until my next visit,' she said. 'The bridges, though. They're nearer?'

'The Forth Rail and Road bridges and the new Queensferry Crossing?'

'Yeah.'

'Yes,' Doyle said. 'You can see them clearly from South Queensferry.'

'That's far?'

'No, a twenty-minute drive.'

'It's twenty to twelve,' Baker said. 'Don't suppose we can get there and back to The George in time for lunch? I promised my nephew Kyle I'd get some views on my iPhone.'

'Of course,' Doyle said. 'We can manage that easily.'

A few minutes later they crossed into the New Town and Doyle turned into Queensferry Street. 'Straight run from here,' he told her. 'Traffic's light this time of day.'

Baker nodded and indicated a shop they were passing. 'Another antiquarian bookshop,' she said. 'Edinburgh seems to have quite a number.'

'A fair few, yes,' Doyle agreed.

'Angie and I visited one in the Greenmarket yesterday,' Baker said.

'You mean the Grassmarket?'

'Sorry, yes. The Grassmarket. Picked up a book on the subject of ghosts.'

'Interested in that sort of thing, are you, Janice?' Doyle said.

'Yes, ghosts, wraiths, spiritualism, anything other-worldly. Angie and I visited Mary King's Close yesterday. Really spooky.'

'So I believe,' Doyle said. 'I've not seen it myself.'

'Quite an experience, I assure you.'

'What was the book called?' Doyle asked.

'Can't remember the title,' Baker replied. 'But it's about a village called Sauchie. In 1960 residents witnessed some bizarre paranormal happenings involving a poltergeist. Seems interesting. Haven't got around to reading it yet.'

'You believe such things exist?' Doyle said.

'Poltergeists?' Baker said. 'Documented evidence points to the possibility.'

Doyle stopped at a set of traffic lights and gave her a sidelong glance. 'What about possession?'

'Malevolent spirits?' she replied. 'Yeah, recorded cases of that, too.'

'Sounds like you're familiar with the subject,' Doyle said.

'Yeah, it's an interest of mine. I'm a member of the Fairmount Amateur Psychical Society in New York State.'

Doyle selected first gear and moved off as the lights sequenced to green. 'You mean you're psychic?' he said.

'A little,' she said. 'Not that unusual, really. All a matter of perception. Some people are more attuned than others.'

'You can tell things about people?'

'Some things, yes. Everyone has an aura, a life force energy field surrounding them. Psychics see the aura as colours. Are able to tune in and read it.'

Doyle's grip on the steering wheel tightened, the whites of his knuckles showing. 'You can see *my* aura?'

Baker gave a little laugh. 'Of course,' she said.

'What do you see?'

Baker studied him for a moment. 'H-mm. Well, everyone's aura consists of two colours, one light and one dark. The predominant colour in your case is red, which indicates concern. The other, light yellow, signifies an unresolved element in your life. I'd say you were worried about something.' She paused, suddenly serious. 'Oh, I can see a vision.'

'A vision?' he exclaimed.

'Yes. A woman. Dark-haired, late forties. She appears concerned.'

Doyle's face drained of all colour. 'Oh, my God,' he said. 'It's my mother. She knows what happened.'

* * *

Sergeant Gavin Hay and his colleague PC Tom Shaw were sitting at traffic lights at Telford Road and Hillhouse Road at Blackhall when the ANPR device in their Traffic car pinged.

Hay nodded to a dark-blue Toyota, which had just passed through the junction on the major road.

'Index match on that Prius,' he told Shaw.

Shaw ignored the red light, switched on the siren and moved off, while Hay simultaneously activated the radio's *transmit*. 'Golf Tango three-nine to control,' he said. 'Outstanding vehicle alert on Toyota Prius. We have a visual at Hillhouse Road approaching the junction of Corbiehill Road. Show us in pursuit.'

Chapter Twenty-one

Doyle heard the siren, checked his rear-view mirror, and saw a police BMW 530d rapidly shortening the distance between them. He floored the accelerator, increasing his speed from just under forty mph to over seventy.

'Your mother knows what, Ray?' Baker said calmly. 'And why are the cops chasing us?'

Doyle braked hard, slowed for a large roundabout and steered the Prius onto the start of the A90 dual carriageway, his tyres protesting loudly as he threw the Toyota into the corner.

'The murdered women,' he said. 'I wasn't responsible. She's got to believe me.' He glanced at Baker. '*You've* got to believe me.'

Baker's demeanour didn't change. 'Believe what, Ray?' she said.

'What I asked you about – demonic possession.'

'You think you've been possessed?' Baker said.

'I don't think it,' Doyle replied. 'I *know* it.'

'The women,' Baker said. 'What happened to them?'

'Laura… it was my hands around her neck, but it was someone else who killed her. Cassie… well, I just blacked out. She was lying there when I came to.'

They were now on a long, straight stretch, the Toyota edging toward ninety. Doyle had executed several risky manoeuvres, passing two vehicles – an articulated lorry and a single-decker bus – on the inside lane. The driver of the latter gave a prolonged blast of the horn as the Toyota flashed by.

Baker glanced over her shoulder and saw the police car was immediately behind. 'Why don't you pull over, Ray?' she said. 'You're gonna get us killed.'

'Not until we get to South Queensferry,' he said. 'We'll stop at a lay-by opposite The Hawes Inn. Give you time. The police won't try anything if there're witnesses.'

'Give me time for what, Ray?'

'To perform an exorcism,' he said, sounding desperate. 'Take my demons away, Janice.'

'Exorcism?' Baker shook her head. 'I've never done anything like that.'

'You're psychic, aren't you?' he said.

'I told you, Ray, I'm an amateur.'

'You saw my mother, didn't you?'

'Yeah, but–'

'Then you'll do as I ask. Some kind of devil's in me, Janice. I need to get rid of it before I harm anyone else — and that includes you.'

* * *

Knox was at his desk when his landline telephone rang. He picked up and said, 'DI Knox.'

'Dave at reception, boss. Urgent call, Traffic Control.'

'Thanks, Dave,' Knox said.

A moment later a voice at the other end of the line said, 'DI Knox?'

'Yes.'

'Sergeant Alistair Reid, sir, Traffic Control HQ. We've found Doyle's car on the A90 approaching the B924 South Queensferry turn off. The senior member of crew, Sergeant Hay, would like to speak to you.'

'Okay,' Knox said. 'Patch him through.'

There was a hum of static, then Knox heard Hay's voice. 'Sir?'

'Yes, DI Knox at Gayfield Square. Carry on.'

'We've been tailing Doyle for the last five minutes, sir,' Hay said. 'He's currently two miles south of the South Queensferry exit.'

'There's someone with him?' Knox asked.

'Yes, sir. Female in her twenties.'

'Her name is Janice Baker,' Knox said. 'An American tourist.' A pause. 'He knows you're following him?'

'Yes, sir. We've had blues and twos on from the moment we picked him up. He increased his speed to around ninety after he joined the dual carriageway north of Barnton. Weaving in and out of traffic, so we pulled back a bit. Didn't want him losing control.'

'Good idea,' Knox said. 'Keep him in sight, but don't crowd him. You know where he's headed?'

There was a moment's silence then Hay said, 'Update, sir. He's just indicated left, joined the filter lane for the B924.'

155

'Heading for South Queensferry?'

'Aye,' Hay said. 'We're about a third of a mile behind. He's swung onto the flyover and joined the B924, two-way traffic.'

'Okay,' Knox said. 'Keep him in sight, but don't attempt to stop or apprehend for the moment. Doyle's a double murder suspect. Unpredictable. I don't want to put his passenger at risk.'

'I understand, sir.'

'And stay on the line, Sergeant; keep me updated.'

'Sir.'

Knox turned to Hathaway. 'The iPhone Doyle and Banks use for their cab work. We've the number?'

Hathaway turned to his computer screen. 'Yes, boss,' he said. 'I have it here.'

'Pass it over, will you, Mark? I have an idea.'

* * *

Doyle glanced in his rear-view mirror. The Traffic car continued to hold back, and was now a half-mile behind. He steered the Prius into a bend, descended a final hill, and drove into the town of South Queensferry.

He passed beneath a latticework of girders supported by ten granite piers, which stretched from the headland towards the first of the Forth Rail Bridge's three cantilevered sections.

A section of roadway near the structure was reserved for sightseers, and it was here he chose to park.

He indicated a dozen or so other vehicles nearby as he switched off the ignition. 'As I hoped it would be,' he said to Baker. 'Not all that busy, but not all that quiet.' He glanced across to The Hawes Inn, where the BMW had just come to a stop. 'And, more importantly,' he added, nodding to the police car, 'Too many witnesses for them to try anything foolhardy.'

'You're holding me hostage, is that it?' Baker said.

'Only till you do as I ask, Janice.'

156

'I've already explained, Ray. I've no experience in exorcism.'

'But you saw my aura,' Doyle said. 'If you can see that, you can surely see something else.'

'Sorry, Ray. I don't know what you mean.'

'Whatever's possessing me; that must also be visible.'

Baker studied Doyle for a long moment. There was no doubt in her mind that he was mentally ill. He'd admitted murdering two women too, so he must be dangerous. Yet, strangely, even though he'd made a veiled threat against her, she didn't feel frightened. And not just because she was in a busy place with police nearby. He genuinely appeared to think she could help him. All things considered, where was the harm in going along with it?

'Okay,' she said. 'If I do as you want, perform an exorcism, you promise you'll give yourself up?'

Doyle brightened visibly. 'Of course,' he said eagerly. 'I'll have nothing to fear then,' he said. 'You see, Janice, it wasn't me. I'm not a killer, couldn't have done such things of my own free will. I'll be rid of my demons, won't I?'

'Okay,' she said. 'You'll need to give me a minute or two. Sit back in your seat, try and relax, I'll do the same. Helps me concentrate.'

Across at The Hawes Inn, Hay and Shaw were sitting in the BMW, engine idling, keeping watch on the Prius.

'What are they doing?' Shaw said.

'Engaged in conversation, by the look of it,' Hay replied.

'He's switched off the ignition, anyway,' Shaw said, noting the lack of fumes from the Toyota's exhaust. 'Doesn't look like he'll make a run for it anytime soon.'

'Couple of pandas in place at the western end of town,' Hay replied. 'Another two Traffic cars have set up a roadblock on the B924 behind us. Paddy wagon on its way from Corstorphine. Won't get far if he does.'

The radio crackled and the pair heard Knox say, 'Still there, Sergeant Hay?'

'Hearing you loud and clear, sir.'

'Doyle still parked opposite The Hawes Inn?'

'Almost ten minutes now.'

'Okay,' Knox said. 'I've got his mobile number. I'm going to give him a ring and find out what the situation is. Possible he's taken her hostage, might try to bargain his way out. That being the case, I've asked for a trained negotiator to be ready. I'll call you back afterwards.'

'Okay, sir,' Hay said. 'We'll standby. Wait till you advise.'

Back in the Prius, Baker turned to face Doyle. 'Okay, 'I'm ready,' she said, adding, 'according to my research, a crucifix is used when undertaking exorcism. Something we don't have. We'll have to improvise.'

'It's okay,' Doyle said. He undid his top shirt button and removed a silver chain, to which a crucifix was attached. 'There's a small one on this pendant, belonged to my mother.'

Baker nodded. 'That'll have to do.'

As he handed her the pendant, the mobile on the dashboard began ringing. Doyle glanced at the iPhone's screen, but failed to recognise the caller and made no attempt to answer.

'Hadn't you better get the phone first?' Baker said.

'It's no one I know,' he replied. 'Probably cops. Ignore it.'

'Thing is,' Baker said. 'If you don't answer, they'll call back. Likely to keep calling till you do.' She shook her head. 'It'll break my concentration.'

'Only one way to deal with that,' Doyle said. He rolled down the window and reached for the mobile. 'I'll get rid of it.'

'No, Ray – don't,' Baker said. 'You promised me if I did this, you'd give yourself up. Get rid of the phone and the cops will rush to the car. If they do that, there'll be no time for me to help you. Better talk to whoever's calling. Explain that you need more time.'

Doyle stayed his hand. 'Aye,' he said. 'You're right.'

He pressed the iPhone's *accept* icon and said, 'Hello?'

'Raymond Doyle?' Knox said.

'Yes. Who's that?'

'Detective Inspector Knox.' A beat. 'Your passenger, Janice Baker. She's okay?'

'Of course,' Doyle replied indignantly. 'Why wouldn't she be?'

'Can I talk to her, please?'

'You don't believe me?'

'I need to check, Raymond.'

Doyle nodded to Baker. 'Say something, Janice,' he said.

'Hi,' she said. 'It's Janice Baker.'

'You're okay?' Knox asked.

'Yeah, I'm fine.'

'Good,' Knox said, then to Doyle, 'Can you tell me why you've stopped where you have, Raymond?'

Doyle ignored the question. 'I want you to instruct your guys to hold back,' he said. 'We need more time.'

'I'm sorry, Raymond,' Knox said. 'I don't understand. More time for what?'

'Janice is psychic. She's going to perform an exorcism.'

'To do what you asked Father Murphy when you visited St Bridget's on Sunday?' Knox asked.

'Aye,' Doyle said bitterly. 'If he'd done as I asked, Cassie Mullen would be alive today.'

Knox let that pass. 'Ms Baker,' he said, 'she's willing to undertake that for you?'

'I'm not forcing her, if that's what you mean.'

'I'd still like to hear her say it,' Knox said.

Doyle glanced at Baker. 'Yeah,' she confirmed. 'I'm doing it of my own free will.'

'Okay,' Knox said. 'How much time do you need, Janice?'

'Two or three minutes,' Baker said. 'Ray's promised to give himself up afterward.'

There was a short silence, then Knox said, 'Okay, Raymond, here's what I'd like you to do. Keep the line open. You can mute the sound while Ms Baker carries out the exorcism if you like. I'd like her to confirm when it's done, though. At that point allow her to exit the passenger door and walk towards the police car. I want you to leave the Toyota then with your hands in plain sight. Remain with the vehicle until officers arrive and take you into custody. Do you understand and agree, Raymond?'

'I do,' Doyle said. 'Provided you wait until Janice confirms the exorcism's been done. No interruptions.'

'We'll wait till we hear from her,' Knox said. 'You have my word.'

'Right,' Doyle said. He reached over and pressed the mute button on the iPhone. 'Okay, Janice,' he added. 'You can begin.'

Baker nodded. 'Before we do, Raymond,' she said. 'You realise it's usual for this procedure to be done by a priest?'

'You're Catholic?' Doyle said.

'I am, yes,' she said.

'I thought so,' Doyle said, and shook his head. 'I've had it with priests, Janice. No, you're psychic and of the Catholic faith. That'll do for me.' He paused, and added, 'Please... begin.'

'Okay,' she said. 'I want you to sit back and relax.'

As Doyle settled back in his seat, she held the crucifix aloft and began:

Prayer to St Michael the Archangel

In the name of the Father,

and of the Son,

and of the Holy Ghost.

Amen...

Chapter Twenty-two

'And Doyle gave himself up okay after the American carried out the procedure?' McCann was saying. 'No drama?'

'No, submitted himself like a lamb, apparently,' Knox said.

An hour had passed since Knox had spoken to Doyle at South Queensferry. The murder suspect had been taken into custody and was presently in a cell at Gayfield Square.

'And Ms Baker,' Hathaway asked. 'He released her as promised?'

'Immediately after the exorcism,' Knox said. 'According to Sergeant Hay, one of the Traffic officers who carried out the arrest, she was quite relaxed about it. Hay offered a panda to take her back to The George, but she refused. Said she'd promised to get some images of the Forth bridges on her iPhone for her nephew. Told him she'd get a black cab to take her back into town afterwards. He's arranged for officers from West End Police Station to take her statement this afternoon.'

'Cool customer,' McCann said.

'Aye,' Knox agreed. 'Maybe just as well, considering what Doyle's capable of.'

'He's been charged yet?' McCann asked.

'Preliminary charge was read to him by desk sergeant Charlie Roker, when he arrived,' Knox replied. 'Because of his mental state, though, Doyle's brief asked for our CMO, Dr Haigh, to undertake an evaluation.'

'Dr Haigh saw him?'

'Yes,' Knox said. 'Decided on sectioning. He'll be transferred to Gogarburn Psychiatric Hospital under section 174 of the Criminal Procedure Act.'

'No likelihood of him being released, I take it?' McCann asked.

'I wouldn't think so. Gogarburn's a category B institution. Depends how it goes at his trial. After charges are brought and evidence given, they may even decide to transfer him to Carstairs. That's category A. Little chance of his release if that happens.'

Knox glanced at his watch. 'Okay, half past one,' he said. 'Not a bad morning's work. Let's hope this afternoon will prove equally fruitful.'

'Simmonds?' McCann said.

'Aye,' Knox said, and turned to Hathaway. 'DCI Collins said he was going to be at St Leonards all afternoon, Mark?'

'Yes, boss,' Hathaway said. 'That's what he told me.'

'Righto,' Knox said. 'I'll give them a ring and confirm. Head up there after lunch.'

* * *

Knox and McCann arrived at St Leonards shortly before 3pm. The civilian receptionist directed them to Room 23, where Knox's tap on the door was answered by a peremptory, 'Come in.'

The detectives entered and saw DCI Collins sitting behind a desk near the window. DI Simmonds was leaning on a filing cabinet to his left.

'Ah, Knox,' Collins said brightly. 'I believe congratulations are in order. You've apprehended your double murderer?'

'The man's in custody sir, yes,' Knox replied.

Collins nodded. 'Good work.' He waved to a couple of chairs in front of the desk. 'Please, take a seat.'

Knox and McCann did so as Collins took out a folder. 'Now,' he continued, 'to the matter in hand. The charge against Sergeant Fulton.'

McCann looked at Simmonds, who remained standing. She detected the hint of a sneer on his face.

'Mr Toomey now claims my colleague encouraged him to falsify his statement?' Collins said.

Knox nodded. 'Yes, sir. Everything Toomey told us is in my report.'

'You accept that Toomey conspired with Gilliland in the commission of the crime?'

'I do, sir, yes.'

'And as such isn't the most reliable of witnesses?'

'I'm aware of that too, sir, yes.'

'You might also acknowledge, DI Knox, that such an individual, given his position as an accomplice, might say anything – even switch testimony when speaking to police? In other words, might tell interviewing officer A one thing, and say something different to officer B?'

Knox glanced at Collins' colleague. 'DI Simmonds is denying that he coerced Toomey into changing his statement?'

'DI Simmonds simply ran with a hunch that Toomey and Gilliland were known to each other, that's all, DI Knox,' Collins said. 'Toomey made a statement that Gilliland's injury was a result of the manner of Sergeant Fulton's arrest, and now says something else.' He tapped the folder. 'I'm throwing it out, I'm afraid. The man's an unreliable witness.'

Knox bristled. 'What about the statement from Mr Lennie, barman at the Regent Tavern?'

Collins shrugged. 'I'm treating that as hearsay, DI Knox,' Collins said. 'And anyway, it's academic.' A pause. 'As of this morning.'

'Sorry, sir,' Knox said. 'I don't follow.'

'Edward Gilliland's out of danger, Inspector. Transferred to a normal recovery ward at the Royal Infirmary. His mother instructed Mr Read, their solicitor, to drop the charges. I reported my findings to my superiors, and it's also been decided that the charge against Sergeant Fulton is unproven. He's reinstated, effective immediately.' Collins patted the file, and added, 'So, you see, the point's entirely moot. The case has been dismissed.'

* * *

The moment they were back in the car McCann clicked her seat belt into place and said, 'I'd an idea Simmonds was off the hook when I saw the expression on his face.'

'Ran contrary to my expectations, and that's a fact,' Knox said.

'What do you think, boss – Simmonds is brown-nosing someone higher up?'

Knox shrugged. 'Maybe. Certainly didn't expect Read to give up on the case that easily, particularly after Lyon's interview.'

McCann nodded agreement. 'Strange that Gilliland's mother decided to withdraw the charge.'

Knox started the car and began the drive back to Gayfield Square. 'Aye, and I can't see that happening just because her son's out of danger.' He paused. 'Wouldn't surprise me if some sort of deal's been struck.'

'You mean promising leniency?'

Knox dipped his head in agreement. 'I think so. Lyon highlighting the subject on Monday ruffled a few feathers. And Simmonds' coercion of a witness, had it been discovered, would've added fuel to the fire. I think it likely Collins or one of his bosses has had a quiet word.'

'Well, Bill's reinstated, so that's something,' McCann said. 'Even if that bugger Simmonds is off the hook.'

'Yeah,' Knox agreed. 'One positive, at least.'

* * *

Fulton was talking to Hathaway when Knox and McCann arrived in the office. 'I was in the middle of gardening when the Chief gave me a ring,' he explained. 'Handed the pruning shears to the wife like they were white-hot. Rushed back in case he rang again to say there'd been a mistake.' He gave Knox a searching look. 'Gilliland's definitely out of danger? His mother instructed their brief to drop the charges?'

'Yes, it's true,' Knox said. 'And good to have you back on the team, Bill.'

'Aye, I echo that,' McCann said.

'Simmonds,' Fulton asked, 'he put his hands up?'

Knox shook his head. 'Unfortunately, no. Looks like some sort of deal's been done. Arlene and I were surprised, to say the least.'

DCI Warburton had exited his office and approached as Knox spoke. 'Surprised me too, Jack,' he said.

Knox turned, slightly startled. 'Sorry, sir, didn't know you were there.'

'It's okay,' Warburton said. 'Hadn't meant to creep up on you.' He gestured to his office. 'DCI Collins phoned not long after you departed for St Leonards. He told you about his decision concerning DI Simmonds?'

'Yes, sir,' Knox said disdainfully. 'The crux of which was that he wasn't prepared to give credence to Toomey's statement.'

Warburton noted Knox's expression. 'I agree, Jack,' he said. 'Pretty feeble. And, to be honest, totally unexpected — from the Collins I knew, at least. The only thing I can say in his defence is that it's possible the decision came from higher up.'

'Did DCI Collins say anything about the charge against Gilliland?' Knox asked.

'Yes,' Warburton said. 'I was coming to that. The Pik-Pak store dropped the charges. When he leaves hospital he's a free man.'

Knox glanced at McCann, who was rolling her eyes. Warburton caught her expression, and said, 'I know, I know. Safe to assume a deal's been done. Quid pro quo, and all that – Gilliland's brief withdraws the charge, and his client goes free.' He shrugged and added, 'Goes against the grain, I realise, but sometimes we just have to accept it.'

Warburton promptly changed the subject. 'By the way, I meant to thank you for bringing in the girls' murderer.'

'Only one cog in the wheel, sir,' Knox said. 'It was a team effort.'

'I'm aware of that, Jack. Anyway, he's out of our hands now, taken to Gogarburn Psychiatric Hospital.'

'Already?' Knox said. 'That was quick.'

'Yes,' Warburton agreed. 'Dr Haigh signed the sectioning order and Doyle was transferred while you and DS McCann were at St Leonards.'

While Knox took this in, the DCI checked his watch. 'Well, it's almost five,' he said. 'If you've nothing else on the books, I think we can call it a day.'

'No, I think we're pretty much done,' Knox replied. He turned to Fulton and grinned. 'Shame to bring you in for nothing, eh, Bill?'

'Wasn't for nothing, boss,' Fulton said. 'Never thought I'd be so happy to see the inside of the office again, even for a wee while. Beats pruning rose bushes any day, believe me.'

* * *

As Knox slid behind the wheel of his car, his mobile rang. A glance at the screen caused him to raise his eyebrows. 'Lucy?' he said.

'Jack,' Carmichael replied. 'Hope I haven't caught you at an inconvenient moment.'

'No,' Knox said. 'Just finished. About to make my way home.'

'Look, I called to apologise for last night. I was completely unreasonable. Only thing to say in mitigation is I was slightly drunk, which tends to make me mawkish.'

'Nothing to apologise for, Lucy. It was me, being presumptuous.'

'That's just it, Jack, you weren't. I was stupid. You were kind, solicitous… and I had a lovely evening. Honestly. Can we start again? Please?'

'Well, I–'

'I told you about my flat at Ratcliffe Terrace?' Carmichael interrupted.

'Yes,' Knox replied. 'Yes, you did.'

'The deal went through quicker than I expected. Got the keys and took possession this morning. Alex Turley was very gracious, gave me time off to deal with it. By this afternoon I'd moved in most of the furniture I had in storage. Also did some shopping. Thing is, I'm having a bit of a housewarming this evening and I'd like you to come.' There was a short silence, and she added, 'Please say you will.'

'Well, like I say, I was on my way home,' Knox said. 'Need to take a shower and change first.'

'That's perfectly okay,' Carmichael said. 'Say seven-thirty?'

'Yes,' Knox said. 'That should be fine. I don't need to dress up? Your housewarming isn't formal, or anything? How many folk will be there?'

'Isn't formal, Jack, so no need to dress up,' Carmichael replied. 'And definitely no other guests. Just you and me.'

Chapter Twenty-three

Gogarburn Psychiatric Hospital – five months later

Dr Andrew Melrose was addressing a group of colleagues in the staff room of an administration building a short distance from the junction of Gogarburn Road and Glasgow Road, eight miles west of Edinburgh city centre.

'I'd like to welcome our newest colleague, Dr Alexis Hamilton,' he said to the assembled group of five men and three women.

The members introduced themselves to the newcomer, and Melrose continued, 'Two others among you haven't been here long, namely Dr Majorie King and Dr Phillip Smythe. So for the benefit of all three, I'll briefly go over the topography of the hospital, before moving on to other business.'

Melrose went to a map on the wall behind him. 'The hospital complex covers an area of approximately twenty-five acres,' he said. 'The perimeter of which, as you can see, roughly describes an oblong, from the East Entrance to the Edinburgh Airport slip road, some four miles to the west. On a north to south axis, the grounds are approximately a mile in width.'

He tapped an "X" on the map near a line marked "Gogarburn Road entrance". 'The admin block is here, at the East Entrance.' He ran his finger to a nearby L-shape. 'The adjacent structure is Freelands House, a maximum-security building. Here the most disturbed patients are housed, currently numbering…' He paused and turned to a bespectacled man in his late thirties. 'Dr Rogers?'

'Thirty-four, sir,' the man replied.

'Yes, thirty-four,' Melrose agreed. 'We've a permanent staff of sixteen nurses dedicated to Freelands House on a 24/7 basis. None of these patients is regarded as particularly dangerous, either to themselves, other patients, or staff. Nonetheless, strict security is enforced. You'll appreciate that Gogarburn is a category B institution.'

'Excuse me, Dr Melrose?' One of the doctors, a red-haired woman in her mid-twenties, had raised her hand.

'Yes, Dr King?' Melrose said.

'Those who might prove unpredictable, what criteria is used for their classification?'

'You mean assessment of a tendency towards violent behaviour?'

'Yes, sir.'

'Forty-eight hours observation by either myself, or my senior colleague, Dr Thomson. Backed up, naturally, by a complete assessment of their case file and the transgression that led to their incarceration. If either Dr Thomson or I have any doubts, they'll be recommended for immediate transfer to a category A institution, most likely Carstairs.'

'I see, sir,' King said. 'Thank you.'

Melrose nodded, turned again to the map, and ran his finger along an undulating thick black line on both sides of which were drawn a number of squares. 'This is the road which leads through the remainder of the complex east to west,' he said. 'The boxes, twelve in number – six on either side – represent the remaining patient quarters. These are single-storey self-contained bungalows, each with four rooms, and it is here that the other inmates are housed. These patients are in various stages of treatment, and are allowed a great deal more freedom to move about the hospital grounds. Most are allowed to aid their rehabilitation by doing light work: gardening, undertaking light property maintenance such as painting, that sort of thing.'

Melrose indicated the western end of the map. 'Up here, beyond the canteen and stores block, we've successfully landscaped a wooded area over the last year or so. Installed a duck pond and added some trout.' He pointed to a narrow line meandering through a series of circles representing trees. 'We're rather pleased with the result. A secluded and tranquil spot where patients can walk, feed the ducks and trout, and take their ease.' Melrose turned and joined the others. 'I'm confident it's proving of enormous benefit in their recovery.'

Dr King raised her hand again. 'May I ask another question, sir?' she said.

'Yes, you may,' Melrose said. 'Carry on.'

'What about security for patients in the bungalows? Isn't it easy to exit the hospital grounds?'

'Very good question, Dr King,' Melrose said. 'As you will have observed, the complex is surrounded by a low wall, with no surveillance on the gate. The reason few patients commit a breach is two-fold. Every bungalow has a resident nurse, and each patient is electronically tagged.'

As King nodded, Melrose reached for a folder and turned to the first page. 'Now,' he said. 'Other business. On Mondays we have a weekly patient progress review. I'd like to begin with one of your charges, Dr Rogers: Raymond Doyle.'

Rogers shifted in his seat and opened a file. 'Yes, sir,' he said. 'Mr Doyle appeared at court three months ago on a double murder charge.' He paused. 'The women, both in their twenties, were killed over a period of ten days. Doyle was brought to us after Dr Haigh, the CMO with Police Scotland in Edinburgh, completed the sectioning order.

'He was examined by Dr Thomson and myself after arriving at Freelands House, where he claimed that at the time of the murders he'd been possessed. Apparently he'd approached a priest and requested an exorcism, but this was refused. Doyle, who was a taxi driver, later abducted a passenger, an American called Baker who claimed to be psychic. She carried it out instead.'

'An exorcism was done by a lay-person?'

'Yes, sir.'

'And he believed this had helped him?'

'At the time he did, sir, yes,' Rogers said.

'Why, what happened subsequently?'

'Dr Thomson and I placed him under observation for a week. Found him to be suffering from ambulatory parasomnia, which manifested in him experiencing blackouts.'

'Really?' Melrose said. 'For the benefit of anyone unfamiliar with the condition, you'd better explain.'

'Ambulatory parasomnia is a blanket term for behaviour which the subject isn't aware of – a sort of sleepwalking,' Rogers said. 'The difference with Doyle is that whilst in that state he became violent. Had no memory of his actions when he returned to consciousness.'

'You conducted tests?' Melrose asked.

'Yes, sir. Dr Thomson and I took sensors and set up a sleep study in Freelands House. We measured brain waves, eye movement, muscle tone, nasal airflow, respiratory effort and oxygen levels.'

'I see,' Melrose said. 'Carry on.'

'Dr Thomson and I were looking for behaviour which indicated that Doyle's account of those blackouts were episodes of sleepwalking. Things like sleep apnoea – where breathing is interrupted – or episodic limb movements –

where arms and legs thrash about as in some sort of fit. In Doyle's case, these signs were easy to find.'

'And your conclusion?'

'That Doyle had carried out the killings while suffering from ambulatory parasomnia.'

'You were called to give your findings at his subsequent court hearing?'

'Yes, sir. The panel decided he remained a serious threat, and recommended a period of incarceration of no less than ten years. Their only concession was that it could be served in a category B institution, rather than category A, which the prosecution had called for.'

'You have him on medication?' Melrose asked.

'Gabapentin 300mg,' Rogers replied.

Melrose nodded. 'How has he responded?'

'Very well, sir. Absolutely no episodes after six weeks of treatment. Normal social interaction with staff and other inmates. A model patient.'

Melrose nodded. 'I see you approved his transfer to bungalow B3 a little over a month ago. I also note he requested to be addressed by his middle name, Martin, and that he's taken his mother's maiden surname, Geeson.'

'Yes, sir. He felt it would help to put his old life behind him, and I agreed. He's grown a beard, too, to complete the change.'

Melrose nodded. 'And he's working in the canteen stores, under the supervision of Nurse Royston?'

'Yes, who's also in charge of bungalow B3.'

'Fine. Good work, Dr Rogers,' Melrose said, and returned to his folder. 'Okay, next case…'

* * *

'I think she fancies you, Martin,' Sam Royston was saying. The nurse and his charge were carrying boxes of supplies into the hospital kitchen, and a fair-haired woman in her mid-twenties had just flashed a smile at Doyle.

He grinned. 'Amy?' he said. 'Yes, I like her, too. We arranged to meet after lunch, take a walk up to the pond, feed the ducks. You don't mind?'

'Of course not, son,' Royston replied. 'As long as you're back at the stores by three-fifteen. I'm expecting a delivery.'

'Thanks, Sam,' Doyle said. 'We can't be any longer. Amy's bus back to town is due at three.'

The pair exited the canteen and went to a VW Caddy, where Royston closed the van's doors. 'What time did you arrange to meet her?'

'When she finishes,' Doyle replied. 'Half two.'

Royston checked his watch and nodded towards the canteen. 'On you go, then,' he said. 'It's almost that now. Don't keep her waiting.'

'Thanks, Sam,' Doyle replied.

Royston nodded and went to the driver's door. 'Mind now,' he said. 'Quarter past three.'

'Won't forget, Sam. I promise.'

Amy joined him at the front of the canteen and minutes later they arrived at a clearing beside the duck pond. Amy reached into a carrier bag and took out a loaf and gave him half. They tore off pieces of bread, which they threw to the ducks, who devoured each morsel hungrily.

'How long have you been here, Martin?' Amy asked.

Doyle thought for a moment. 'Around five months,' he replied. 'You?'

She gave a little laugh. 'Only four weeks.'

'You like it?'

'Working as a catering assistant?' She shrugged. 'It's a job.' A short pause and Amy added, 'What I meant when I asked how long you'd been here, was how long it might be until... until you're able to leave.'

He shrugged. 'Up to the doctors, really. They seem quite happy with my progress.'

She nodded. 'Sorry, Martin, it's none of my business.'

'No, no,' he said. I don't mind. I was in a bad way for a while. Headaches, sleeplessness, that sort of thing. Made me quite…' Doyle caught himself. 'Well, I'm much better now.'

They finished feeding the ducks, and Doyle indicated a bench at the other side of the path. 'We can sit for a few minutes,' he said. 'You've enough time?'

Amy glanced at her watch. 'Uh-huh,' she said. 'My bus isn't due for another fifteen minutes.'

They sat in silence for several moments, then she said, 'I've had troubles of my own, to be honest.'

'Really?'

'Yes, went through a divorce. Messy. My husband was cheating on me. Arrived home early one day and caught him in bed with a woman who lives two doors away.'

'Oh.' He looked at her again. He couldn't be sure but, up close, he thought there was something strangely familiar about her.

'Which part of town was this?' he asked.

'Where we were staying?'

'Yes.'

'Gilmerton Dykes. I left him and went back to stay with my mother. In Northfield.'

Doyle felt something akin to an electric shock run up his spine. 'Northfield?' he said, and almost immediately saw a flash of light in his peripheral vision.

Oh, God, no. Please, don't let her say it. Don't let it be true.

'Yeah, Northfield,' she confirmed. 'The name I'm known by here at the hospital, Nuttall, is actually my married name. My maiden name is Madden.'

The light had become more intense now, and he knew he was about to experience a blackout.

'My Christian name isn't Amy either,' she continued. 'It's Amanda. Amanda Madden…'

The End

List of Characters

Officers based in Edinburgh and elsewhere:

Detective Inspector Jack Knox – head of the Major Incident Inquiry team based at Gayfield Square Police Station, Edinburgh

Detective Sergeant Bill Fulton – Knox's partner, second member of the Major Inquiry Team

Detective Sergeant Arlene McCann – third member of the Major Inquiry Team

Detective Constable Mark Hathaway – fourth member of the Major Inquiry Team

Detective Chief Inspector Ronald Warburton – senior detective at Gayfield Square Police Station

Detective Inspector Edward (Ed) Murray – forensics officer based in Edinburgh

Detective Sergeant Elizabeth (Liz) Beattie – forensics officer and Murray's assistant

Detective Chief Inspector Reginald Collins – Professional Standards Department, Gartcosh Police HQ, West Central Scotland

Detective Inspector Dave Simmonds – Professional Standards Department, Gartcosh Police HQ, West Central Scotland

Detective Inspector Thomas (Tam) Guthrie – Leith Police Station

Sergeant Gavin Hay – Traffic patrol officer

PC Tom Shaw – Traffic patrol officer

Others:

Alexander Turley – pathologist, based at Cowgate Mortuary, Edinburgh

Lucinda Carmichael – pathologist, based at Cowgate Mortuary, Edinburgh

Laura Winter – Canadian, first murder victim

Mrs Catherine Winter – Laura Winter's mother

Cassandra Mullen – second murder victim

Father Ryan Murphy – priest at St Bridget's Church

Peter Irving – verger at St Bridget's Church

Edward Gilliland – thief at Pik-Pak store

Bernard Wilkie – security guard at Pik-Pak store

Mrs Carter – proprietress, Sea View Guest House

William Carter – Mrs Carter's son

Jackie Lyon – presenter, Lowland Independent Television

Ms Elena Harper – Ms Lyon's personal assistant

Mr Miles Read – Gilliland's solicitor

Mr George Middleton – genealogy specialist

Mr George Banks – 2Ucabs driver

Mr David Toomey – Pik-Pak shelf-stacker

Mr Doug Lennie – Regent Tavern barman

Nurse Beck – Eastern General Hospital

Dr Mellor – Eastern General Hospital

Angela Perry – American visitor

Janice Baker – American visitor

Dr Andrew Melrose – Gogarburn Psychiatric Hospital

Dr Majorie King – Gogarburn Psychiatric Hospital
Dr Adrian Rogers – Gogarburn Psychiatric Hospital
Nurse Sam Royston – Gogarburn Psychiatric Hospital

If you enjoyed this book, please let others know by leaving a quick review on Amazon. Also, if you spot anything untoward in the paperback, get in touch. We strive for the best quality and appreciate reader feedback.

editor@thebookfolks.com

www.thebookfolks.com

MORE FICTION BY ROBERT McNEILL

All the books in this series of DI Jack Knox detective novels are free on Kindle Unlimited and available in paperback!

The Innocent and the Dead (Book 1)

One girl is found dead – strangled in the woods. Another, the daughter of a rich, well-connected businessman, is kidnapped. Unassuming detective Jack Knox must solve these two cases. But the Edinburgh crime-solver will have a hard time getting his superiors to accept his unconventional methods. Will he gamble too much?

Murder at Flood Tide (Book 2)

When a young woman's body is found, the nature of her killing leads detectives to believe the murderer may strike again soon. The race is on to find him, but he has covered his tracks well. DI Jack Knox's investigation is impeded by a disgruntled officer from another force. Can he solve the case and collar the culprit?

Dead of Night (Book 3)

When a philandering French college lecturer is killed and unceremoniously dumped in a canal, DI Jack Knox soon discovers there is no shortage of spurned lovers and jealous husbands who might have done it. He sets about collaring the culprit, but will his efforts be thwarted by unfair complaints made about the investigation?

Noughts and Crosses (Book 4)

After defrauding wealthy investors of a serious amount of money, a financial advisor is found dead on a residential street in Edinburgh. DI Jack Knox must tread carefully to follow the trail that might lead to the killer. But will the events that ensue prove too much even for him?

A View to Murder (Book 5)

When a student is found dead in the crags in Holyrood Park, DI Jack Knox must make sense of her friends' conflicting stories about the events that led up to her death. But his boss risks putting a spanner in the works when Knox is asked to act as a go-between in a deadly drugs sting.

Don't Cry, Darling (Book 7)

The Edinburgh major crimes team is on high alert after a shooting at a card game leaves three people dead. But the officers must divide their focus when the daughter of a prominent figure goes missing. Can DI Knox catch her abductor before the unthinkable happens, and stop a dangerous killer in his tracks?

OTHER TITLES OF INTEREST

NEAR MISS by Traude Ailinger

After being nearly hit by a car, fashion journalist Amy
Thornton decides to visit the driver, who ends up in
hospital after evading her. Curious about this strange man
she becomes convinced she's unveiled a murder plot. But
it won't be so easy to persuade Scottish detective DI
Russell McCord.

Available free with Kindle Unlimited and in paperback!

THAT MUCH SHE KNEW by Linda Hagan

A woman is found murdered. The same night, the office pathologist Jenny Norris goes missing. Worried that her colleague might be implicated, DCI Gawn Girvin in secret investigates the connection between the women. But Jenny has left few clues to go on, and before long Girvin's solo tactics risk muddling the murder investigation and putting her in danger.

Available free with Kindle Unlimited and in paperback!

*Sign up to our mailing list to find out about new releases
and special offers!*

www.thebookfolks.com